THE CASE OF THE CHINESE BOXES

Suddenly there was a flash of gold and a hand grabbed mine. I felt the pain as my fingers were sharply crushed into the palm of my hand. Then just as abruptly the pressure was released. It all happened in a second. I'd been caught off guard. I didn't even have time to see who'd done it.

I scanned the faces in the crowd, not even sure what I was looking for. Eyes that might quickly avoid my gaze, eyes that might give me a glint of recognition, a flash of gold in the darkness of the park, a figure stealing away into the shadows?

I scanned the whole area but all I saw were happy families.

My assailant had disappeared completely.

Carefully I uncurled my fingers. Thin crescents of blood were forming where my nails had dug into the palm. I opened my hand further and saw that a fortune cookie had been pressed into it. I separated the broken pieces and picked up the strip of paper on which the message was written.

If you chase the dragon beware the sting of its tail.

Also by Marele Day

The Life and Crimes of Harry Lavender
The Last Tango of Dolores Delgado

The Case of the Chinese Boxes

Marele Day

CORONET BOOKS
Hodder and Stoughton

For G.M., who pushed the envelope

First published in Australia in 1994 by Allen & Unwin

First published in Great Britain in 1994 by Hodder & Stoughton

First published in paperback in 1995 by Hodder & Stoughton
A division of Hodder Headline PLC

A Coronet paperback

10 9 8 7 6 5 4 3 2 1

All characters in this publication are fictitious and any resemblance to real persons, living or dead, is purely coincidental.

British Library Cataloguing in Publication Data

Day, Marele
Case of the Chinese Boxes – New ed.
I. Title
823 [F]

ISBN 0 340 61346 7

Printed and bound in Great Britain by
Cox & Wyman Ltd, Reading, Berkshire

Hodder and Stoughton
A division of Hodder Headline PLC
338 Euston Road
London NW1 3BH

'You are a woman. You are invisible.'

I turned at the sound of her voice and we looked at each other evenly, eye to beautifully made-up eye.

The heat was on. And it wasn't just the temperature.

The address hadn't been difficult to find—the ground floor flat of a corner block. I turned into the car-lined street. One of the cars was a white Merc with black tinted windows but I guessed that wasn't too unusual for Woollahra. I walked up to the ground floor flat and peered in through the screen-door. It was not quite a residence and not quite an office either. I had the distinct impression the premises had been hired for the occasion. I looked at my watch—two minutes past the appointed hour and no-one about. I tried the handle of the screen-door. It wasn't locked.

The interior was plush; galah pink and grey which would fade in a few years to the status of flared trousers. A pink corded sofa and a glass-topped table the size of a tennis court. A charcoal coloured desk in one corner with a swivel chair either side.

I looked at the areas people didn't normally look at. The corners of the ceiling and the corners of the floor. The pink, grey and black paintings which I discovered were fixed to the wall. The rug that came up easily and revealed nothing.

The phone on the desk rang. I waited around but still no-one came. I didn't imagine it would be for me but I couldn't over-come the natural urge to answer it.

It was for me. A woman's cultured voice telling me that Mr Chen would be there presently and to make myself comfortable.

I settled into the pink corded sofa. It was hot outside and not much better in here. On the tennis court table was a stack of magazines and a coffee tray. The tray was ornate and gold and looked like it shouldn't have been left unattended. On the tray was a pot of coffee. Put here fairly recently, judging by the heat of it. Surrounding it were some exquisite Chinese cups, thin as eggshell and decorated with miniature dragons breathing fire. The coffee smelled inviting. I felt like Alice in front of the DRINK ME bottles. I hesitated, but like Alice I was curious. I relaxed a little. I wasn't exactly twelve years old and nubile. I poured some coffee into a cup and put it to my lips. I took a mouthful and rolled it around in my mouth a little, letting the taste-buds do a fast analysis. All I could taste was coffee, an Italian mocha blend. I waited a while but I didn't get any smaller. Nor did I see any white rabbits. But I was getting increasingly curious about the mysterious Mr Chen. Someone else had made the initial appointment for him. And had rung to make sure I was here.

And now he was keeping me waiting.

I wasn't even sure Chen was his real name. It sounded like the Chinese equivalent of Smith or Jones. Maybe he was a well-known businessman who wanted to keep his business with me quiet. People usually do.

I flicked through the stack of magazines—*Far Eastern Economic Review*, *Asiaweek*, *South China Morning Post*. It all looked pretty dry and fiscal. There were photos of clean-shaven men in business suits. They looked pretty dry and fiscal as well.

I got up and opened the window to let some air in, then went back to the sofa and sat fanning myself with the *South China Morning Post*.

I heard a car door slam and straightened up the magazines. I hadn't heard a car pull up.

A man and a woman entered and I stood up to meet them. They looked alike, maybe a brother and an older sister. I wondered if they were the advance guard. Both had finely sculpted faces and were immaculately dressed. But there were differences. The guy tripped on the rug as he came in and the woman didn't.

Silently the woman closed the door and window. Then she sat down in the same spot on the sofa that I'd occupied. The seat was probably still warm.

I thought about opening the window again but it was hardly the thing to do. I was on their ground—if they could take the heat so could I.

The young man sat in one of the chairs at the desk and with a somewhat floppy hand movement, invited me to take the other. Little beads of perspiration formed on his upper lip as he opened his mouth to speak.

'Good morning, I am Mr Chen.'

Mr Chen was not quite what I'd expected.

'Claudia Valentine,' I said, offering my hand over the desk. With my other hand I turned on my pocket cassette recorder.

'You were not followed here?' he asked.

'Not unless you saw someone while you were sitting in the car.'

His hand shot up to smooth hair that was already slicked down with gel. He glanced quickly at the woman on the sofa, startled at having been found out but also impressed. He turned back and steadied his milky fingers in prayer position. Mr Chen was a nervous boy.

'We have invited you here to discuss a rather delicate matter.' He cleared his throat and shifted in his chair. 'My family has business interests in Chinatown.' Money was always a delicate matter, especially when you had a lot of it. 'You may remember the bank robbery in Chinatown a few weeks ago, safety deposit boxes.' Especially when a lot of it went missing.

In the quiet holiday period after New Year the Chinatown bank robbery had scooped all the headlines. Then it had dropped mysteriously out of the media except for a short follow-up in a Sunday newspaper which stated that only half of the eighty victims of the heist had come forward to declare their losses. Hardly surprising considering that the contents of safety deposit boxes were 'safe' from the prying eyes of the Taxation Office.

The heist wasn't going to do the private eye business any

harm either. Maybe this case would be the first of many that would come my way. I liked the efficiency of doing one lot of work for several clients. It was neat. Very neat and the research was recyclable.

These thoughts went through my head in the time it took to nod to Mr Chen. Yes. I remembered the bank robbery.

He continued. Many of the families in Chinatown lost a lot of money in that robbery but more importantly they lost irreplaceable family heirlooms. 'Ours was such a loss. A small item but. . .' He looked towards the sofa and changed tack. 'It is not the monetary worth, it is the great sentimental value, a family heirloom.'

He took a photo from the inside pocket of his Armani jacket and handed it to me. It was a photo of a key.

An antique key made of gold. With a tubular shaft and at one end six teeth. It must have been an intricate lock that key fitted. But that wasn't what commanded my attention.

It was the dragon at the crown of the key—the same fire-breathing dragon that decorated the coffee cups.

'This key is one of the items that went missing during the robbery. We would like you to find it. The thieves may still have it. We would like you to find them and make them an offer. A considerable offer. For return of the key, no questions asked.'

He leant back in the chair and breathed a sigh of relief, as if he had been rehearsing for weeks and the performance was now over.

'What makes you think I can succeed where the police have so far failed?'

'You are a woman. You are invisible.'

I turned at the sound of her voice and we looked at each other evenly, eye to beautifully made-up eye.

The heat was on. And it wasn't just the temperature.

It would be like trying to find a needle in a haystack.

But I liked long odds.

They were waiting for my answer.

I nodded my head.

'So. We are agreed?' said Mr Chen.

'We are agreed,' I echoed, turning back to him.

The woman came over to the desk and smoothly retrieved the photo I was still holding. 'No need to burden you with this,' she said, as if doing me a favour by lightening my load.

I didn't really need the photo; there weren't too many keys like that around. If it was still around.

'What's it the key to?' I asked.

She smiled indulgently. In a minute she'd be telling me to run along and play. 'It is not the key to anything, it is a family heirloom. Charles?'

Mr Chen dived into his pocket again and produced a cheque. For a thousand dollars.

'This will be satisfactory for the moment?'

'That's fine.' I was trying to sound like thousand dollar cheques happened to me every day.

'You will of course give us progress reports and we will be of whatever assistance we can.' She handed me a business card. 'You can contact my son or myself on this number.'

Son? She was his mother? When we got a bit friendlier I might ask her what skin creme she used. If she was the sort of person you got friendly with.

I looked at the card. The Red Dragon. A restaurant, the proprietor of which was Mrs Victoria Chen.

I waited in my car long enough to see Charles and Victoria Chen get into the white Merc with the black tinted windows, then I drove to Randwick to pick up my kids. It was late in the day. I would start earning my thousand dollars tomorrow. Tomorrow the school holidays would be over and the kids would be returning to their father. It was usually a slack period for me—even crims go on holidays—but if a job cropped up, Mina was a more than willing babysitter. That suited me fine. I liked to keep my kids well out of the way of my business.

I parked in the driveway of the old suburban house and walked round the back. I could hear the kids squealing and came round the corner to see them firing at each other with water-pistols.

'G'day, Mum,' said Amy breathlessly.

'Mum!' shouted David, and squirted the pistol at me. I twirled around but he got me anyway.

Mina stirred under her big sun-hat and coughed a throaty cough as she eased herself up on the banana chair. Her white slacks were rolled up to her knees, showing the legs that had once been compared to Betty Grable's. They still looked good. Freshly painted red toenails peeped out of the white sandals. Even at home my mother dressed as if a Hollywood agent might drop in on her. I stubbed out the cigarette smouldering in the ashtray. There was a sizeable pile of butts there already.

'Hello, love,' she greeted me, 'how did the interview go?'

'Got the job.'

'Good girl!' she exclaimed, patting me on the arm.

I'd given up trying to convince my mother that meetings with clients weren't auditions. Though the idea of a chorus line of private investigators strutting their stuff was an interesting proposition.

Legwork was all part of the game and I fancied my high kicks would make an interesting variation to the average gum-shoe shuffle.

'Want a drink?' I knew it wouldn't be alcohol. My father had drunk enough of that for all of us. 'I've got some. . . David, stop that!' she shouted.

I turned around in time to see a rather wet cat sprinting into the neighbour's yard. David looked at me with his lips tightened, not sure which way the wind would blow. I raised my eyebrows at him and he tightened his lips even more, trying to suppress the grin. Amy crept up behind him, water-pistol at the ready.

'. . . juice in the fridge,' Mina finished her interrupted sentence.

'Gotcha!' shouted Amy as David yelped. The game reeled on.

'I'll get it,' I said. 'Amy, David, you'd better wind things up if you want to go down to Darling Harbour tonight.'

'Can we go back to your place first?' asked Amy.

'Why? You got a pressing need to tidy up your Lego?'

'I wanna see that man in the pub. The one with the black teeth that talks to himself.'

'Well he'll still be there when we get home.' There was no fear of missing George. He was the first to arrive and the last to leave.

'You know what, Mum? David reckons he's our grandfather.'

Mina and I looked at each other. This time it was our turn to tighten our lips.

It wasn't to suppress a grin.

My ingenuity as a child-minder had been tested during these long summer holidays. As the part-time parent I felt my role was to fill the weeks together with such memorable occasions that when the kids went back to their father's place in Queensland there would be enough sparkling memories of the bright city lights to last them till the next visit.

Tonight all the lights would be on.

We were on our way to the Lantern Festival at Darling Harbour. Once a spectacular dream in an architect's eye, it had become just another shopping mall, big and brash, as sanitised as laundered money, but the kids stared at it wide-eyed.

I had, against all principle, consented to a ride on the monorail and sat quietly as the kids pressed their noses to the glass and looked at the star-spangled banner of Sydney.

'It looks like my train-set at home,' said David as we returned to the Harbourside shopping mall and walked down the steps.

'Yes, well it is a toy. A big boy's toy,' I said, and headed them off towards Tumbalong Park.

All around the park area were conventional Chinese lanterns, red tassels swaying in the breeze; and there were other decorations—spangly red fish and Chinese junks made of cellophane and bamboo. The moon, full and fat, floated like a balloon in the light night sky. Lit up beside it was the white needle of Centrepoint Tower.

A good-sized crowd had gathered in the park for the Lantern Festival. A portable stage was in place and we squeezed in right up close, sitting on plastic bags on the night-moist grass so that those behind could see over our heads. The average age of the crowd was about seven.

While waiting for the ceremony to begin Amy and David eyed up other kids the way children do, aware that they were in a world of peers and that the adults were outnumbered. Many of the kids were Chinese. I wondered whether the Lantern Festival tugged at their roots or if it was just another tourist attraction. The prize for the winner of each section of the lantern-making competition was a bank account with a deposit of a hundred dollars. I was glad the banks of Chinatown still had something in the coffers to offer children.

There was a sudden hush as the compere appeared. With his shining yellow robe and mitred hat he looked like a bishop. Underneath, white trousers and white shoes peeped out. The bishop's cheeks were rouged and there were touches of make-up around the eyes and mouth. He held the portable microphone like a true professional: 'I can hear the full moon, you're so quiet. Can you all hear the full moon?'

'Yes!' the little liars ready to believe this conjuror's magic shouted in one resounding high-pitched boom.

He announced the winners in each age group and they paraded their lanterns around the stage, subtly directed by the magician's assistant who also hauled off those who, dazzled by the lights of precocious fame and fortune, lingered too long. The winners got a bank account and fortune cookies as well. Then all the kids got fortune cookies, including David and Amy who held out their hands to the nice Chinese lady like dogs begging for biscuits.

They came back to me unrolling the cheap thin paper. 'You will be pretty and rich,' read Amy through a shower of fortune cookie crumbs. 'You will have good for-tune,' read David.

'It's good luck,' I said when he asked me what four tunes it meant.

Suddenly there was a flash of gold and a hand grabbed mine. I felt the pain as my fingers were sharply crushed into the palm of my hand. Then just as abruptly the pressure was released. It all happened in a second. I'd been caught off guard. I didn't even have time to see who'd done it.

I scanned the faces in the crowd, not even sure what I was looking for. Eyes that might quickly avoid my gaze, eyes that might give me a glint of recognition, a flash of gold in the darkness of the park, a figure stealing away into the shadows?

I scanned the whole area but all I saw were happy families. My assailant had disappeared completely.

Carefully I uncurled my fingers. Thin crescents of blood were forming where my nails had dug into the palm. I opened my hand further and saw that a fortune cookie had been pressed into it. I separated the broken pieces and picked up the strip of paper on which the message was written.

If you chase the dragon beware the sting of its tail.

Instinctively I gathered my children to me.

'What's yours say, Mum?' asked Amy.

'The holidays are over. It's time for you to go home.'

The waiter brought slices of square brown bread with equally square pats of butter, and a large Greek salad. The seafood restaurant in Erskine Street was rapidly filling up with business people who provided the bulk of the lunchtime clientele. The service was fast, the fish fresh and the price right.

I speared a baby octopus while Carol watched the manoeuvre suspiciously.

'A good vet would have that swimming in half an hour,' she said.

I looked twice at the little creature but ate it anyway, biting decisively so the tentacles wouldn't choke me on their way down.

'You think that octopus has more right to life than the lettuce you're munching on?' I said to Carol, who had recently begun a stint of vegetarianism. 'Look at those pale little leaves, that's probably it's heart you have in your mouth right this minute.'

'You've always got an answer for everything, haven't you, Claudia?' she replied coolly.

'Only the easy ones, I come to you for the hard ones.'

'Well the National Bank job is a hard one for us as well. The biggest bank haul in Australian history, the most professional job since the Great Bookie Robbery, and the trail's gone cold. The cash is untraceable and the valuables are probably melted down now or in Hong Kong. You don't fancy a little trip there, do you?'

'Not if I can help it. Sydney's my patch and I'm sticking to it. Better the devil you know.'

Carol's eyebrows swam together under her thick bangs of hair. 'There might be some devils here you don't know. That bank job doesn't have any signatures on it that we can decipher. I wish you luck. Better luck than we've had anyway.'

Carol was often cagey about police information but on this one it was full co-operation. The police hadn't been able to get anywhere on it. And if a private investigator with ways and means could uncover something that the police, tied by legalities, couldn't, so much the better.

As we stood up to leave she handed me a list of those who had come forward to declare their losses. The Chens weren't on it. The bank had refused to give the cops a full list of their safety deposit box holders. I was pleased to know that some institutions still stuck by their guarantee of the individual's right to privacy.

At the cash register the cashier knew precisely what we had ordered and we paid accordingly. There was a long line of office girls and boys waiting patiently for take-aways beside the grill plates and vats of boiling oil where chips sizzled. Fast chefs with dirty white aprons worked away at the vats as if they were conducting orchestras. I didn't know how they could do it in that heat.

'Jim Campbell of the Breaking Squad might be of help,' Carol said when we were out in the street. 'I'll let him know to expect you, shall I?'

'Thanks Carol, you're a gem.'

She looked at me suspiciously. Carol was never one to accept compliments graciously.

'This communication channel is two-way. Any leads that you come across you'll pass on to us of course.'

'Of course,' I repeated.

'You wouldn't like to start by telling us who your client is?'

'That's right Carol, I wouldn't.'

'Even as an act of faith?' she asked hopefully.

'Faith we have in abundance. It's facts that are a bit thin on the ground. Besides, knowing who my client is won't lead us to the robbers. It's fairly routine: they've lost something, I've got to find it.'

'Where are you off to?' asked Carol when we got to the corner of Erskine and York.

'Ultimo. What about you?'

'Back to work. You remember work, don't you? You must have seen it on TV.'

'Feeling nostalgic? Still wish you were out in the streets, Carol?'

'Not at all,' she said abruptly. 'I like the feel of my padded leather chair, and the huge desk keeping the sleazebags at bay. I need to know there's money coming in every week now that I have a mortgage as well as a leaky roof over my head. What are you going to do when you get too old for this game?'

'I'm fit, I'm not going to grow old. Don't have a mid-life crisis on my behalf.'

The lights changed and Carol started to cross. 'Don't forget Jim Campbell.'

'Thanks Carol, see you later.'

I knew why Carol was so keen for me to use her contacts—so she could keep an eye on me. But I had a few contacts of my own.

The air hung low and heavy. It was one of those late January days from childhood. It was always like this on the first day of the new school year, back in school uniform with white blouses that Mina bleached to get out the rings of sweat. The heat sat on you like a fat furry bear.

It was the bear that influenced my decision to take a cab. I rarely brought my car into the city these days. Any more carbon monoxide and you could commit suicide by just sitting at the traffic lights and breathing.

When I arrived in Ultimo, journos back from long lunches were making their way into the newspaper building like worker bees re-entering the hive. They had an intensity about them, frayed at the edges, of those who write for a living and to a deadline, hoping to God the city would throw up a new story each day so they wouldn't have to make a lost dog sound like a major political event.

I followed them in, past the bays that in the early hours of the morning would be loading their stories into trucks bound for the country, but which now lay idle and empty.

I took the lift to the sixth floor and asked for Brian Collier. There was nothing to fan myself with in the reception area so I just sat and quietly sweated.

It wasn't long before I saw Brian making his way towards me. For once he had taken off the tweed jacket that seemed to have been stitched on surgically. He was wearing a beige coloured shirt that may have once been white, and a wool tie. The shirt sleeves were rolled up to just below the elbows and revealed age spots on the hefty forearms.

I stood up and we shook hands. He wasn't the sort of man you kissed every time you saw him and I wasn't the kind of woman who gave them out lightly. I always imagined there was a transfer of information in that handshake, that I was taking in years of the city's stories through the whorls and lines of the palms.

And of course there was the connection with Guy, too. Those hands had been around my father's shoulders, propped him up, maybe wrestled a bottle or two from him.

'Air-conditioning broken down again, has it?' I asked, as we wandered down the maze of corridors.

'Yes, and we'll all be following suit if they don't fix the damn thing soon.'

We stopped outside an office with his name on the door.

'Very impressive,' I said, 'they've moved you out of the classroom into the principal's office.'

'About bloody time too. I've nursed this building through three coats of paint and as you can see they don't do it very often.'

Becoming senior features writer hadn't made Brian any tidier. I removed a pile of papers from a chair and sat down.

'How's your mother?'

I wasn't really convinced by his light-hearted tone of voice. I'd always wondered about Brian and Mina. I had a sneaking suspicion that long ago, when I had been too young to notice, he had fallen victim to the charms of those Betty Grable legs and never quite got over it. All my mother had to say on the matter was that Brian Collier was a 'family friend', and that he'd been a great source of comfort to her through 'all that business with your father'.

'She's fine. Still smoking like her life depends on it, but otherwise fine.'

Brian eyed me suspiciously. 'You haven't become one of those born-again non-smokers, have you?'

'I never smoked in the first place, and no, it doesn't worry me if other people do. It's just that Mina. . .well, sometimes she sounds like a steam-engine chugging up a hill.'

A shadow of concern passed across Brian's face then he laughed it away. 'Talking about chugging up hills, you didn't come all the way up to the sixth floor just to see my office, did you?'

'Not entirely. What's the word on the National Bank robbery?'

'The Great Chinese Take-Away? It wasn't my story. I can take you to our library files then if you have any questions I might be able to direct you to the appropriate source. What are you looking for, the gold or the drugs?'

'Drugs?'

'Yeah. Word has it that as well as gold there was heroin stored in them there boxes. Mind you, it's worth more than its weight in gold. Word also has it that certain parties held a summit meeting.'

'Certain parties?'

'Some of the big boys round town—white and yellow. The upshot of it was—get the bastards. The word is out. They can't go to the police and they can't go to their own kind. Whoever did it has as much protection as a sparrow in a windstorm. If they're still in the country, that is.'

'They have to be,' I said determinedly.

'You know, or you want?'

'Got a feeling about it. They're still here.'
'You after the breakers or an item?'
'Item. But one thing may lead to the other.'
'An you can succeed where the cops have not?'
I smiled at Collier and let the question answer itself.

I expected to have to search through back copies in the library looking for news of the robbery, but the librarian had beaten me to it. Collier introduced me to her and told her what I was after. She looked like a nice woman, efficient but friendly. She got out a file headed *1988, Crimes, Australia*, and flicked through it. A slim file, but the year had only just started. She came to *Robberies* and lifted out the folder that said *National Bank, Haymarket*, and handed it to me.

'The photocopier's over there if you need to use it.'

It was something of a bonus on this hot afternoon, in this hot stuffy building, to have some of the material already pre-digested. At least I'd been saved the trouble of flicking through trees of newspapers looking for the meaty bits.

Fifteen minutes was enough to photocopy the lot.

I returned the folder to the librarian and renegotiated the labyrinth back to Collier's office.

He was on the phone, or rather the phone was on him, nestled on his shoulder, the way they do it in the movies. I'd never been able to manage it myself, it kept slipping under my chin.

It didn't really suit Collier, the phone looked too toy-like, but it did allow the hand that wasn't taking notes to offer me a seat.

I sat. And started reading through the photocopies.

The bank had been broken into over the New Year weekend, the sound of the revels covering the explosions as the strong-room door was blasted. This was 1988 and two hundred years of white man's history were being celebrated with particularly loud bangs. It was estimated the breakers spent up to forty-eight hours in the bank and came out at regular intervals to drink in nearby hotels and establish alibis. Did the cops know this or was it just the media spicing up the story? I think I would have taken in a thermos and a couple of sandwiches and stayed there for the duration.

As soon as Collier put down the phone it started ringing again. He picked it up and made a thin-lipped smile at me. It was one of those afternoons. One of those afternoons when more civilised countries have siestas.

There were photos and diagrams of the bank. The facade facing George Street looked unassuming in one photograph, but another, an aerial view, revealed that the bank extended the width of the block back to Sussex Street. The photo was taken in daylight and there were cars in the street. The same cars that had been there when the break was going on? Positioned across the cars in the photo was the caption: HOW THEY DID IT.

Step by step.

1 Entered through construction site.

The site could only be seen from the aerial view, a pit hidden by facades.

2 Climbed scaffolding.

3 Used ladder to reach window.

In another of the clippings, where a diagram took the place of the aerial photo, these two steps were reversed.

I was aware of Collier's phone ringing again and a soft curse. An office of one's own was not without drawbacks. I mimed departure and left.

By the time I hit Broadway the traffic, never a pleasure along that particular stretch, was a sea of hot gleaming metal. Everything shimmered in a brown haze. The faces in the cars were tight, silent and closed. They had their minds set on automatic and were thinking of the cold beers waiting at home.

I'd nearly walked to Glebe Point Road by the time a vacant cab came along. The driver wasn't impressed with having to cross the lines of traffic to turn right and he wasn't much of a talker. That suited me fine. All I wanted to do was follow the breakers into the bank, carrying the oxy-acetylene equipment, wondering about the security guard. No. They'd have known when he did his rounds, would have timed it for that.

4 Walked downstairs. Gang member used extension ladder to enter fourth floor window. He then ran down two flights of stairs to force a second floor window to allow the gear to be brought in.
5 Breaking tools taken to basement vault.
6 Broke through security doors.
7 Blasted way into safety deposit box strongroom.
8 Rifled boxes.
9 Attempted to blow cash-safe but triggered off alarm.

Therein the drawings and steps ended. More of the story was constructed based on paraphernalia the thieves left behind.

There was a photo of the vault door with the metal pulled back like paper to reveal the lock. There was also a photo of a safety deposit box. It looked like a crumpled shoebox. It had been photographed in the street; there were out of focus cars behind it. There was a sticker on the side of the box with writing on it. Through the black and white dots of the newspaper photo the words were indistinguishable.

'Bloody good job that one.'

I looked up. We'd rounded the Crescent, passed the timber mill, and were grinding on to meet the White Bay traffic. The inevitable Bush Dance sign hung on the wire fence, shot through with bullet holes so that the wind wouldn't lift it and sail it away. Beatrice, the lady who sells newspapers in her Balmain football socks, was slipping a paper out of her bundle and in through a car window. A good way to supplement the pension if you didn't mind weaving in and out of the fast lane.

'Pardon?'

He turned around and leered at my lap where the photocopies were nestling. My skirt suddenly felt very short.

'That bank job. They'll never get 'em, you know. They'd be out of the country by now, living it up in Rio.'

'That was the Great Train Robbery,' I said coolly.

'Must be the place to go then,' he said, winking.

I got out two blocks from the pub and walked the rest of the way.

I got a couple of bottles of Cascade from Jack and took them up to my room. I opened the french doors to let some of the heat out, and with Vince Jones crooning to me from the cassette player, had a more careful look at the clippings.

The estimates of the haul ranged from ten to a hundred million dollars worth. I'd never seen a million anything except for grains of sand.

My old university training got the better of me and I found myself taking notes. There was just one story but a million ways of telling it. Maybe rearranging the pieces might show up a pattern hitherto unrevealed.

eighty safety deposit boxes rifled
cash, gold, securities, jewellery, family heirlooms (heroin? gold keys?)
gang may have received inside help—gang member may have posed as customer to get bank layout
oxy-acetylene equipment and gelignite, other equipment left behind—theft of explosives previous month from Batemans Bay
highly skilled and very professional
former safecracker: 'It's been an easy go for years and I don't think that much planning would have gone into it.'
fair chance most of the haul will end up overseas—Hong Kong, Singapore, but 'there are people who collect these sorts of things here, maybe the offenders had these contacts. Don't think criminals are fellows with scars on their cheeks with one eye looking this way and the other looking that.' (Det. Chief Inspector Kevin Parsons)
alarm set off but security guard found 'nothing untoward' in the bank's main cash-vault on ground floor, reset alarm, if he had gone down a single flight of staits he may have caught them red-handed, 'brazen robbers bypassed guard . . . by using the lift to travel from basement to first floor'
victims not declaring contents of boxes
a group of Sydney criminals 'discussed in a Darlinghurst hotel a plan to find the bank robbers and use torture to persuade

them to part with the proceeds of the robbery—a bizarre twist' (summit meeting Collier referred to?)

Mr Henry Ming Lai, who replaced the murdered Mr Stanley Wong as chairman of the Dixon Street, Chinatown Chinese Committee said 'We have no information or knowledge of how many Chinese had boxes or the contents that were in them.'

Several of the 'valuable items' had been listed. A jade Buddha and phoenix, numerous gold and platinum bracelets inscribed with dragons, birds and Chinese characters, several 1937 Australian pennies worth at least $50 000, unset stones including diamonds, rubies and emeralds.

They didn't mention any heroin.

Nor did they mention a gold key with a fire-breathing dragon.

After two bottles of Cascade and both sides of Vince Jones, I had several pages of notes but little else. Nothing much happens in the underworld without someone getting a whiff of it. But as time went by the trail was getting colder. The gang might not be part of the underworld at all. Maybe they were guys who had nine to five jobs and only robbed banks on weekends. They were smart, organised and tight-lipped. Agile enough to climb scaffolding, strong enough to carry heavy equipment. I wasn't ruling out the possibility that the guys were women.

Why bother jemmying open eighty safety deposit boxes? Why not simply blow the safe? Were they in fact looking for something specific? A gold key? No-one would go to all that bother. Would they?

I took Vince out of the cassette player and slipped in the interview with the Chens.

'...sentimental value, a family heirloom...' I tracked forward. '...A small item but...'

But what?

I played that bit over, listening to the gaps between the words, listening to changes in the tone of his voice. Tried to picture him sitting there saying it.

Him sitting there, and the woman.

A simple head movement from the woman on the sofa would have been enough to pass the message.

I played the whole interview over again, including Mrs Chen's final words. I got the message now—don't complicate matters, stick to the script, only tell her what's absolutely necessary.

A faint breeze was coming through the french doors but the temperature wasn't getting any cooler.

I gathered up my notes and the empty beer bottles. Then I noticed a damp patch near the bed. I looked more closely and saw a gun. A green water-pistol—Amy's. I picked it up and felt the last of the water drip out on my hand. I wiped the pistol dry and put it away in the box that held the rest of my children's things. Soon the damp patch would dry and disappear.

I looked around the room. Usually I called this neat and tidy. At the moment it looked empty and bare.

The phone rang. It was Steve. Did I want to go out?

I did.

The Malaya had gone upmarket. What used to be a pale green room with laminex tabletops and lino had now expanded into an up and downstairs, with a ritzy bar and black carpet with tiny red dots on it. But the memu hadn't changed in years. I think the beef curry had been handed down through generations. During my student years I had eaten a beef curry here every Friday night. We used to think it was the in-place to eat. Some people still did.

The waiter placed margaritas in front of us. They looked deliciously cool, the colour of an Arctic sea.

'How was it at the airport?' Steve asked.

'OK,' I said, half-heartedly picking bits of salt off the rim of the glass.

'Yeah. I know.' He knew. He had Ulrike with him only once a year. At least I had David and Amy four times a year and the phone calls to Queensland were more frequent than Steve's calls to Germany.

'Amy asked if she could be penfriends with Ulrike,' I said.

'Yeah, good. It might help her English if she has another correspondent apart from me.'

The beef curries were the same as they'd always been, like a good book you couldn't put down, but our minds weren't really on the food. Having mostly absent kids was something we had in common. We understood what it felt like and it was the way I at least had chosen it, but still the post-departure gap was there. We ate the meal in silence and sweated out the curry.

The rest of the restaurant was buzzing with conversation, flying off the walls and the hi-tech chrome. I wondered how many of the people sitting here had lost something during the robbery, how many of them had detectives out there searching through haystacks. Not many. The only Chinese person in the Malaya was the cashier.

We went back to Steve's place and sat in the jungle courtyard drinking champagne. The night was still hot and steamy.

He moved his chair closer. I took off my shoes and put my feet up on his lap and began lightly pressing his groin with my toes. He circled his fingers on the tops of my feet, then began brushing his lips on them. By the time he got to the inside ankles my loins were stirring.

'My, what long legs you have, Ms Valentine.'

'Yes,' I purred, 'and they go all the way up.'

'So do I,' he said. 'So do I.'

There are two ways of finding a needle in a haystack. Either you tread on it accidentally or you go through the stack straw by straw. Until an accident happened I'd have to go through it straw by straw.

Most of the gold dealers are in Martin Place. There are trees and flower stalls in Martin Place and a modicum of oxygen. It's a place for people and the difference is discernible. They sit on smooth seats, eating sandwiches out of paper bags and listening to the lunchtime jazz concert. Others quietly read newspapers.

I walked into the GPO to buy a stamp. There was a queue of backpackers at Poste Restante. I remembered when I had stood in the middle of foreign cities waiting for mail or money from home. Wearing cut-off jeans, silver jewellery, sandals and a backpack, idly talking to other travellers, comparing hostels, good beaches and whether you were suffering yet from the local bugs. Things hadn't changed all that much except that now I was on the other side, a part of the scenery. I didn't mind, I'd spent my time in the queue.

I stuck my stamp on the letter addressed to the kids and walked out into the sunlight.

None of the gold places in Martin Place is on street level. Gold isn't street business, it's discreet.

The lift came eventually and let out four men in business suits talking numbers and percentages. Men in suits always remind me of schoolboys, even the ones with moustaches. You could still pick out the bully, the yes-men and the wimps.

I got in the lift and touched the square of light that indicated the second floor.

When the doors opened again I stepped out onto grey carpet. It was quiet up here but not the sort of quiet you find in a church. It had no smell, no breeze. It was like having cotton-wool in your ears.

I came to a steel grey door and tried the handle but the door was locked. Then I noticed a small buzzer to the right that invited me to press. I accepted the invitation and through the glass panels either side of the door watched a neat but unimaginatively dressed girl approach. Why go to all the trouble of a steel door if you had glass panels either side of it? I suppose it allowed you to see whether the person at the door had a stocking over the head and was carrying a machine-gun.

As she let me in she let out a Chinese girl wearing a thin gold chain around her neck. I noticed the chain because hanging from it was a small gold key. The door closed and separated us before I could see whether the key had a dragon on it. I looked back through the glass panels but the key and the girl had disappeared.

The place was both a shop and an office. There was a counter beneath which were display cases of gold jewellery—chains, brooches, earrings, cufflinks, and keys with '21' and '18' on them. There was the same dove grey carpet on the floor and the same feeling of cottonwool in the ears. Behind the counter and filing cabinets were windows that looked out over part of the city, a silent city from here, that you couldn't hear or smell.

To the left was a desk and seated behind it a man in a navy-blue suit and gold-rimmed glasses. He glanced at me but soon went back to discussing business in soft tones with another man who had his back to me.

'Can I help you?' asked the girl who had let me in. She had shoulder-length brown hair held back with a pale pink clip. She wasn't exactly twin-set and pearls but I was willing to bet her mother was.

'I hope so.' I showed her my ID. She looked at it then back to my face. Neither of us commented. There was no need. I wasn't the first private detective who'd come to a gold dealer.

She didn't invite me to sit down but that was all right. Both of us hoped I wouldn't be there long enough for sitting.

'Do you buy gold items?'

'Yes.'

'What happens to them?'

'They're sold for scrap.'

I had a feeling in my stomach as if a small furry animal had stretched out in its sleep. I saw the drop of gold that was the key melting in the heat and becoming an indistinguishable part of an ocean of gold. I looked at the keys in the display case. 'Wouldn't you just resell them?'

'We don't have a licence to sell second-hand goods,' she said primly.

No, it didn't exactly look like a pawn shop.

'So all these are new?'

'Yes,' she said.

'How long do you keep an item before it gets scrapped?'

'About a day.'

That little furry animal started stretching again. But things were pretty hot out there, maybe it was too soon for the thieves to start getting rid of their haul.

'Do you keep a record of the gold you buy for scrapping?'

'For a time. We fill in a form for the smelters. And we have the client's name, address and phone number.'

'Do you check up on these?'

Her attention was waning. I was beginning to take up her time.

'Not usually. Unless there's a reason,' she said, shifting her weight from one foot to the other.

I described the Chens' key to her.

'Come across this lately?'

'No,' she said.

'You sure? You can remember without checking the files?'

'It's my job to remember,' she said. 'This isn't the first time I've answered a set of questions from people in your... profession.' She turned up her nose as if to avoid an unpleasant smell.

'You mean you've had enquiries about this particular item?'

'No, but others. It's the National Bank robbery, isn't it?'

I smiled. 'If it turns up, or any information about it, would you let me know?'

I handed her my card.

'Yes, Ms Valentine.'

She edged me towards the door. I got the feeling I was the sort of person who reminded her of the seamier side of life.

The steel door closed with no sound other than the lock meshing with its other half and I was on the other side.

I **was meeting** Lucy in the Chinese Gardens and to get there I had to walk across Darling Harbour. Despite the date palms there was not enough cooling greenery. Painting the roof green doesn't do the trick. The green and blue roof panels of Darling Harbour were hardly distinguishable from the sky and the glare was ferocious.

From the outside the Gardens had the appearance of a miniature walled city, with the characteristic oriental roofs curling up their eaves. Despite the walls, the Gardens looked less daunting from this angle than the tall city buildings looming behind them.

I entered, along with a fairly steady stream of tourists. In the vestibule was a sign describing the area as the Garden of Friendship. Also in the vestibule were two security guards though the insignia on their police-blue shirts said 'rangers'.

A plaque with gold lettering described the Gardens, and their history.

> On a fine day when the sun is shining, on a moonlit night or at the break of dawn, a walk through the Gardens enjoying the visual delights will leave one amazed at the boundless panorama. A fondness for it lingers and thoughts of leaving are forgotten. Here in this garden generates the warmth of a friendship which will endure for a thousand springtimes.

All well and good, but the opening times were 10 a.m. to sunset. You could hardly enjoy a moonlit night or break of day in here unless you were willing to scale the wall.

I took off my shoes to feel the cool of shaded cement. I could probably live in these Gardens if they weren't right next door to Darling Harbour.

Most of the other visitors to the Gardens were European but some weren't. I guessed if I went to China the sight of a kangaroo would be a shot in the arm for homesickness. The eucalypts in San Francisco always were.

I walked round to the Reading Brook Pavilion. In the rock-pool on the way were black and red carp. There was also an empty Fosters can. I sat down in the Pavilion and looked upward through the brackets which made cut-outs of the sky. Through a wide space I could see up to the Gurr, Clear View Pavilion, the highest point of the Gardens and, with its three tiers, the most exotic. *The altitude of Clear View can go as far as beyond the cloud.* I watched the people going in and out of it. They didn't stay long, just long enough to look at the hanging lantern then down the steps carved in rock where they disappeared from view.

Except one.

A smallish man who looked like a hood. He had a Mexican bandit moustache, sideburns, and hair that hung over his forehead. He was doing something unusual with his hand, as if straightening his tie. But he wasn't wearing a tie. He was looking out across the Lake of Brightness. His hand in that odd position, two fingers straight out, two bent. Was he signalling to someone or just watching? *Spring seems to be hidden among the dense shade of a thousand trees.* The sight of him made the gradens seem less restful and shade turned to shadow.

'Hey Claudia! Why couldn't we have met in a nice cool bar like normal people?'

I turned abruptly to see Lucy plonk her bag on the seat. I grinned broadly at her. At least if there were two of them there were now two of us. Despite her cheeky face and slight build she could whip an opponent twice her size.

'We're not normal people. Besides, doesn't it remind you of the old country?'

'I was born in Surry Hills. We didn't have a lot of Chinese

gardens round there.' She looked around, taking in the view. 'Quite pleasant,' she commented, 'if you like this sort of thing.'

'Let's hope it stays that way,' I said darkly. 'How are things at the hospital?'

'I dropped everything the moment you rang, including a rather large patient we're treating for alcohol allergy. Can you imagine? You'd become a hermit or something, wouldn't you? If you didn't die of boredom first. What do you mean, "let's hope it stays that way"?'

'Have a look up at the Gurr.'

'I'm looking.'

'What do you see?'

'A three-tiered Chinese pavilion on top of a man-made mountainette. A stream of tourists and a little boy picking his nose and flicking it into the water. What am I supposed to be seeing?'

'An Asian hood.'

'What do they look like?' she asked innocently.

'OK, Lucy,' I said like a parent who'd overindulged a child.

He'd gone. Now he could be anywhere. *Bamboo shadow entering through the curtain. Nightingale hidden in greenery*. Lucy would say I was paranoid. There was no reason for me to think the man with no tie had anything to do with me. But he was up to something. I felt like some fresher air.

'Let's walk.'

'But I only just got here,' protested Lucy.

'We'll walk slowly. Watch out for men straightening their ties when they aren't wearing one. Like this.'

I put my hand on my chest with the forefinger and little finger extended in the way I'd seen the hood doing it.

'You've been watching those Bruce Lee movies again, haven't you? And if you go round Chinatown doing that sort of thing you're liable to have those fingers chopped off.'

'Who's going to chop them off?'

'Red Pole men. Triad street-fighters.'

'Tell me about it.'

'You want to know about that, join a kung fu club. The

standover merchants train there. He who can use his arms and legs as weapons is more persuasive than he who can't.'

'Old Chinese proverb?'

'Australian fact of life. You know that.'

We kept walking. *Nightingale hidden in greenery.* We knew, Lucy and I, what those kung fu boys could do. Certain close contacts with them were lethal and they could use the cover of a crowd to brush against you. To crush a message into your hand maybe? A swift blow to the throat could rupture the cricoid cartilage and suffocate you immediately. Blows to certain other parts of the body could cause death in a few days. And it didn't have to be blows. A finger applied with the right kind of pressure would do the trick. We all knew how Bruce Lee died.

We passed the Hall of Longevity and the Dragon Wall. Two dragons vying for the pearl of prosperity.

'What's this Chinese fetish for dragons?' I asked Lucy.

'They make better pets than cane toads,' she said. 'Besides, Chinese aren't the only ones with a thing about dragons. What about that goofy green St George dragon?'

I made no comment and Lucy eased up on the jokes.

'They can mean just about anything you like. From the forces of nature right up to the emperor. You're walking over one right now. There's a huge dragon living under the ground. No, it's not some fairy story,' she said, seeing my reaction, 'it's good common sense. Before my father bought the place in Surry Hills he called in the *fung shui* man. The guy said the house was in a good position—halfway down a hill, nestled in the belly of the dragon. So we bought it. Circular Quay, on the other hand, has bad *fung shui*. Too exposed to the elements right down there on the water. The worst place to live is on top of a ridge—the dragon's head.'

'What about its tail?'

'That's not so good either, the tail can do a lot of damage.'

If you chase the dragon beware the sting of its tail.

I didn't think that message had anything to do with buying houses. What did it mean? That the dragon on the Chens' key could land me in trouble? That if I started investigating I would be tailed, and the tail would sting? Maybe it was just words playing tricks. The words all fitted together neatly but they may not have had anything to do with what was really happening out there.

'Tell me about the Chens.'

'Why don't I tell you over lunch.'

'In Chinatown?'

'God no. I know where you can get some real food—in Cabramatta. You might find it interesting. Your car's not going to seize up if you drive west of Victoria Road, is it?'

'I think we'll manage.'

'I've got to go out there anyway this arvo. Some meeting about community health. I'd much rather be chauffeur driven in your Daimler than go in the boring old train.'

'Yes, I know.' Lucy had sucked me in yet again.

I felt better in the wide open space of Tumbalong Park than in the confines of the Gardens. *So scattered that one can ride a horse there, so dense that even a needle can hardly be seen.* I thought again about the man with no tie. Maybe the Chens were monitoring my activities. I didn't like the idea. I like working alone. If they were sewing a shadow onto me I might very well trip over it.

'So tell me about the Chens.'

'Which ones?'

'You can start with Victoria.'

'She's inscrutable.'

I looked at Lucy's deadpan face. Then she burst out giggling and put her hand over her mouth to cover it. The discipline and mindfulness of a warrior and a laugh that sounded like a little bell. Even Bruce Ruxton couldn't fail to be charmed. She pulled her face together again.

'What does she do?'

'Lots of things. Runs the Red Dragon restaurant in Dixon Street, for a start.'

'Yeah, and what else? Gambling clubs?'

Lucy screwed up her face. 'Possibly. She runs just about everything else. She's on all the social committees, does good works. The family owns property in Chinatown, she's fairly influential, the power behind the throne sort of thing. Since her husband died she's been trying to train her son to front for her, but despite looking delicious he's a bit of a wimp.'

'When did her husband die?'

'John Chen met with an unfortunate accident some months ago.'

'This hasn't been Mrs Chen's year, has it?'

'The year of the Dragon is always a time of change.'

Of course, this would have to be the year of the Dragon.

'It's more than just that,' Lucy continued. 'There is some . . . instability in Chinatown. Something's going on down there. There are fights, murder even. We haven't had that since the good old days. I don't know, maybe it's these newcomers from Hong Kong, those that don't want to be around for the change of management in 1997. Power bases are shifting. Certain influential "businessmen" are moving out to established Chinatown communities throughout the world, and of course Australia has such a lovely climate. Things grow so well in the heat.'

I knew by Lucy's tone of voice what sort of 'businessmen' she meant. The same sort of 'businessmen' we had here already. As long as you had $500 000 ready cash to invest not many other questions were asked.

'What sort of unfortunate accident did John Chen meet with?'

'He fell on a knife.'

'How come it didn't make it into the newspapers?'

'Hush money maybe. Chinese like to keep themselves to themselves. They shipped the body back to China. Very traditional. The emigrants always wanted to go back to China once they'd made their money in New Gold Mountain. Most times it was like Mr Chen. Back in a box.'

'And a nice long way away from possible autopsies.'

'The death was so inconvenient, John was just about to buy into the antique market.'

'You know an awful lot about them for someone who never sets foot in Chinatown.'

'Only what I hear around the dinner table when I attend a

family dinner—which is as seldom as possible. Lots of tourists round this time of year—and aren't they handsome!'

I turned to where she was looking. On a park bench sat a man with a camera. It had a zoom lens. As he casually raised a magazine to his face a gold watch glinted. I had a flash of déjà vu. And it wasn't just the fact that I also casually raised magazines to my face when doing surveillance work.

When Lucy and I were about five metres away from the bench he put the magazine down and started walking away. Not hurrying away, just strolling.

Something about him reminded me of James Bond. It wasn't the fact he was handsome and wore a well-tailored dark suit. It wasn't the bright yellow handkerchief in the jacket pocket or the black kung fu shoes. It certainly wasn't the fact that he was Chinese.

I picked up the magazine he'd left behind. It was *Rolling Stone* and had Tom Cruise on the cover. But that wasn't what I found most intriguing. It was the headline: TRIADS: THE FULL STORY.

I flicked it open to the appropriate page to find CHASING THE DRAGON.

> The Chinese call it chasing the dragon; you pour a thin line of heroin along a sheet of alfoil, light a match underneath and inhale through a paper cone down the line as the heroin burns and the sickly-sweet smoke hits the back of your throat.

Chasing the dragon. Was that the message? Stay away from drugs? It hardly seemed relevant. But there might be something else in the article that was.

We walked at some distance behind the man till he disappeared into the arcades of Darling Harbour.

'Cute bum,' said Lucy, 'though I prefer blonds.'

'Hmm,' I said absent-mindedly.

How could he wear a suit in this weather and still look that cool? He wasn't even sweating and the trousers still held their crease.

That's what reminded me of James Bond.

Cabramatta was as close as I've been to Asia without actually leaving the country. But I felt foreign long before I got to Cabramatta; I felt foreign at Five Dock. From there on it was red bricks and fibro. I had entered the western suburbs. The city I knew like the back of my hand dropped away and I needed the Gregory's.

We drove through Bankstown. I thought of Carol. Bankstown was where Carol's childhood had withered away and died. The way she presented it, Bankstown was the end of the earth. Cabramatta was even further out.

We drove for miles and everything looked the same.

Finally the highway passed over Cabramatta railway station. 'How do we get in there?' I asked Lucy.

'Do a loop.'

After the railway bridge we turned right and descended into the heart of Cabramatta.

It was the reversal of westernisation. Here easternisation had taken place. The buildings were that make-it-square-and-put-a-fence-around-it architecture characteristic of fifties-style Australian suburbia. But the signs were straight from the Orient. Kim Do Electronics, Tan Hung Meats, the Bing Lee Centre offering the Biggest Bargains This Side of Hong Kong. There was Dr Van Huoc Vo, surgery, beside Tai Huyuk, acupuncturist. From a doorway that said Snuker Bilija Pul you could hear the sounds of snooker balls clinking. The CES was subtitled Trung Tam Tim Viec and the State Bank, Nga Hang.

It wasn't only the signs, it was the contents of the shops and the way things were arranged in them. Every second shop seemed to sell fabric, with rolls of it stuck into bins making a colourful disordered display. Disordered to my eye not yet attuned to the underlying rationale. Everything shouted simultaneously, like a chorus of five-year-olds all singing a different song.

Lunch was well underway when we entered the restaurant. There was a sudden arrest in the atmosphere and all eyes were on us, as if a duck had wandered into a chook-yard. A waiter was cleaning off a table that had been recently vacated, one near the kitchen—probably low on the pecking order, but the only one free. I felt conspicuous enough just standing there, let alone trying to walk out again. We sat down on green vinyl chairs.

'We have only noodles,' said the waiter.

Lucy said something to him and he nodded his head and went off.

'You learnt Vietnamese up there in Surry Hills?'

'Cantonese. Works wonders. I've got us some duck to go with the noodles.'

The restaurant had red and gold bordello style wallpaper and red tasselled lanterns hanging from the ceiling. There was a calendar, a day out of date, from the Chinese Buddhist Society, and a clock made in Canada in the shape of a maple leaf. Between us and the kitchen was a small cupboard with the door taken off. It was a shrine. It was the thought that counted and I'm sure it impressed Buddha as much as a twenty-foot gold statue of himself. There was a drawer above it where the waiter casually flung the dish-rag he'd been cleaning our table with. The inside of the cupboard glowed red; in the back left corner a red electric light bulb was sitting on top of a candlestick. Behind were some Chinese ideographs and in front, incense sticks and an offering of two plump mangoes. In the kitchen sat an old lady looking out at the world, or what was left of hers. She had her feet on a little footstool. She sat so still she could have been a statue.

The waiter came back with the noodles, duckling, and two forks. He hovered about while I picked up the chopsticks already in place and started lacing the noodles around them. 'There are forks,' he said. 'Thank you,' said Lucy, and took them. She started in with the fork. 'I like a bit of iron in my diet,' she said, 'better than plastic.' I persevered with the chopsticks. I felt like I was onstage in front of a thousand people with my pants down.

After a while the other lunchers got bored with watching and went back to talking. It was relaxing to be sitting in total linguistic isolation. To hear sound without meaning. They were probably only talking about operations, marital problems and what was wrong with the car but it was nice not to have to take it in.

We finished with jasmine tea.

Lucy walked off to the Community Health Centre and I started wandering the streets. I went into a supermarket that sold everything. There were packets of fragrant rice and monosodium glutamate, bras spilling out of a bin alongside men's shirts. There were warty cucumbers, long sticks of lemon grass, banana leaf packets of sticky rice, green pawpaw, coriander and other fresh herbs. Deeper into its bowels I discovered some unidentifiable dried matter in leathery brown halfshells. I think it was dried bird embryo. I quickly turned away and looked for something more pleasant. Tins of lychees. Instead of Letona the brands were Dragon Bowl, Twin Elephants, Heaven Temple.

I bought some fresh herbs and left. It was late afternoon when I got back out on the street and the day shift of shoppers was being replaced with the night shift of young dudes cruising. The boys were no more than sixteen, wearing jackets with the sleeves rolled up, and hair that had a lot of time spent on it. There were some girls, mostly accompanied, with nowhere near the peacock strut of the boys.

Then I saw him. The man with no tie. And I wasn't even looking for him. He was coming out of the snooker hall. I saw now why he had been making funny hand signals in the Chinese Gardens—he had two fingers missing. He was with another man who looked like he spent a lot of time in snooker halls. They got into a car and drove off. I took note of the number-plate.

I climbed the stairs to the snooker hall.

The sound of the balls clinking stopped immediately I entered. The room was full of young guys in jeans, holding cues. Some of them had dragons tattooed on their forearms.

But one didn't. Nor was he young or holding a cue.

He was sitting at a table with two other men who looked like minders. They weren't especially big, they just had that air about them. Propped up against the table was a walking-stick.

The man wore an old-fashioned pin-striped suit and a black hat that obscured most of his face. On his hand was a gold signet ring. I noticed the hand because it was resting on a large pile of money. Maybe they were having a quiet game of poker. But I couldn't see any cards. He made no attempt to hide the money, nor did he even look up. He had no reaction to my appearance there whatsoever.

One of the minders came over to me.

'Can I help you?'

'Just looking,' I said.

'Private club. Members only. Sorry,' he said, as if there was nothing he could possibly do about it.

Sure.

The balls on the snooker tables made no sound and neither did the men standing beside them. The cues would make ideal fighting sticks but I didn't have one.

I nodded. My curiosity did not extend to being killed over it. I didn't really feel like a game anyway.

As I walked down the stairs I couldn't help thinking about that man in the black hat. As far as everyone else was concerned I stuck out like a sore thumb. But for him I might just as well have been invisible.

I walked to a central food hall and ordered some shaved ice. There was a choice of green, red, yellow or white to go with it. I settled for yellow and white. They turned out to be chewy mango and lychee.

I was just about to take out the *Rolling Stone* when a tall red-haired security guard came over to my table. I put the magazine away again. The memory of the taxi driver commenting on my reading material was still fairly fresh and I didn't want to be caught out again. The guard was eating fish and chips. He was the only other European in sight. He didn't look as though he was enjoying his job.

'You like that stuff?' he asked.

'Very pleasant.'

'You're not from round here, are you? What brings you to this part of town?'

'Just visiting. What goes on around here that they need a security guard?'

'Anything you'd like to imagine and more,. But that's none of my business and I don't want it to be. As long as things are quiet in here I'm happy.'

He sat down. I hadn't asked him to join me, and the smell of the fish and chips interfered with the taste of mango and lychee. But if he wanted conversation he was going to get it and it wouldn't be just him asking the questions.

'What goes on in the snooker hall?'

'Snooker. What do you think?'

'Not a front for anything?'

'Everything here is a front for something. But I don't get to hear about it. And I'm not curious. It's a good way to be.'

'Do you like this beat?'

'Not particularly. But it's better than going into the city every day. That's where you're from, isn't it?'

'How can you tell?'

'Not hard. The way you're dressed and that.'

'Do you think anyone else has noticed?'

'Probably.'

'Anyone that I should be worried about?'

'Got someone in mind?'

There was just enough wariness in his voice to stop me asking about the man in the black hat.

'No, just curious.'

'Curious is not a good way to be.'

'So you said.'

'It was advice, not a passing comment.'

'Am I boring you?'

'Not yet. But it's probably a good idea not to hang around. You're not one of them and you don't exactly look like a tourist.'

'Next time I'll bring a camera.'

'Is there going to be a next time?'

'Not in the immediate future but you never know.'

'Yeah,' he said, 'you just never know.' He threw his fish and chip paper into a nearby bin. 'I've been working this beat for three years and you know what? I don't know any of these people. Sure, I say hello and goodbye and how's business but beyond that... you know what I mean?'

'Maybe the uniform scares them off.'

'Well that's what it's designed to do. Scare off the shoplifters and stuff like that. That's good, saves me the heavy-duty stuff.' He stood up. 'Been nice talking to you.'

Before he came round again I was on my way back to the car to wait for Lucy.

I sat in the car with the windows up and the doors locked. I didn't feel all that comfortable in Cabramatta and I didn't want to be interrupted while I read the Triad article.

> The dragon has another meaning in Chinese slang; the Dragonhead is the leader of a Triad, the Chinese version of the Mafia.

The article gave a brief history of Triads, named names and dated dates, gave an outline of the Triad hierarchy—the Red Pole in charge of fighting; the Straw Sandal, the administrator; and the White Paper Fan in charge of ritual and promotion. It mentioned a man called Lo Chi Wing (alias Pedro Jong), the Australian Dragonhead who was deported in 1985.

> Since Lo's departure the Triad has continued its operations unabated, with its new Dragonhead a prominent and respected businessman in Sydney's Chinatown.

I was startled by the sound of someone tapping at the window.

It was Lucy, making signals for me to open the door. I leaned over to the passenger's side and let her in.

'God, it's so hot in here,' she said, waving her hand in front of her face. 'What have you been doing, reading dirty magazines?'

'Something like that,' I said, starting the engine.

'Well, how did you like it?' Lucy asked, when we were back on the highway.

'Saw the man with no tie,' I said.

'Sure. There's lots of them in Cabramatta.'

We didn't speak again till we were back in the city.

Jack was eating a toasted ham and cheese sandwich that he decorously referred to as his dinner. George, of the black teeth which had so fascinated my children, and a few other regulars sat at the bar halfway through schooners, reading the newspaper or staring into space. It would be a good ten minutes before any re-orders. Slow drinkers but steady. Only not so steady at closing time when they climbed down off their perches and walked stiffly out into the night air.

'When was the last time you had any greens, Jack?'

'November, 1963. The day Kennedy got assassinated.' He took another bite of the sandwich and signalled me to wait. He had something for me.

'Had a bloke in here looking for you. Said he'd be back. He left this.' Jack felt his pockets, mumbling to himself, 'Where did I put the damn thing? Oh yeah, with the postcards.' He went to the area beside the till where he kept a board of postcards from regulars who had actually managed to leave not only the pub, but the country.

'Not a bad likeness,' he said, handing me a photo.

It was a photo of two people I knew. In a place that I knew. Lucy and me at Darling Harbour. Taken only this morning. I was still wearing the same clothes.

That furry animal stretched out again and clawed at my stomach.

'What did he look like, this guy?'

'Young, Asian, well-bred.'

'Was he wearing kung fu shoes?'

'Can't see the feet from this side of the bar. You want to see him if he comes back?'

'He seem all right?'

'Polite. Not apologetic though. Polite but sure of himself. Chinese, spoke with a pommie accent. Have to be polite with that combination, wouldn't he?'

On the flickering television above the bar the familiar face of a newsreader appeared. Jack turned up the volume and the regulars lifted their noses out of newspapers and towards the screen.

'. . . in Chinatown early this afternoon. Ellis Wong, a martial arts expert, was thought to have been an enforcer for the 14K Triad in Sydney. Police believe this audacious daylight killing to be related to a feud between the 14K and a rival Triad faction . . .'

My mind may have been pole-vaulting to conclusions but when I heard the word Triad I saw the image of the man with no tie standing on Clear View Pavilion. While Lucy and I were still in the Gardens he could have walked the short distance to Chinatown and in some quiet back street carried out the killing. Back to Cabramatta to pick up his pay then driven home. A good day's work well done.

It was too late now to ring Bernie and get the car numberplate checked out.

But it was never too late to ring Carol.

As I turned the key in the lock my phone started ringing. It was Jennifer, the girl from the gold shop. There'd been an enquiry about a key. She thought it only fair to tell me. It was from a Chinese detective, ID issued in Hong Kong. She thought it only fair to tell him also that there'd been a previous enquiry. She also thought it fair, since she hadn't told him my name, that she didn't tell me his.

I thanked Jennifer for her call and told her I'd remember her in my will. She begged my pardon but I said it didn't matter.

As soon as Jennifer had signed off I called Carol.

'What's your interest?' she asked. 'Oh,' I replied breezily, 'I wondered if it had anything to do with the National Bank robbery.' She didn't think it did. 'You got anything to tell us on that score?' she asked. I didn't. I cast my line again into the Chinatown killing. She said as usual no-one had seen anything. Even in reasonably broad daylight. I said I might have. She found that very interesting. I asked her if the victim had been wearing a tie. She said no. I asked if he'd been wearing kung fu shoes. She said what is this, twenty questions? I said no. I told her I'd seen a man acting suspiciously in the Chinese Gardens. She asked what I'd been doing there but I said it was irrelevant. I said I'd seen the same man later that afternoon in Cabramatta. She asked what I was doing in Cabramatta. I said it was irrelevant. I said it was a long shot and probably had nothing to do with anything but it might be worth asking a few discreet questions around the place. Check out the snooker hall. I asked her if she could tell me any more about the victim. She gave me a lot of bland stuff which would be appearing in the next press release.

One piece of information wasn't bland. It stuck up from the surrounding landscape like Mount Vesuvius.

Ellis Wong, martial arts expert, had a day job. He was a waiter. At the Red Dragon.

I sat by the phone but I wasn't looking at it. I was looking at an imperfection in the glass of the french doors, a small bubble like the ones you get in ice, a bubble I often looked at when I needed to concentrate or let my mind put order to an overload of information. Threading the bits of it on string, like beads in a necklace.

I could just see a glimmer in the gathering darkness when there was a knock on the door. I hoped it wasn't a gentleman from Porlock.

'That Chinese bloke's back,' said Jack. 'Want to see him?'

'Send him up. If I'm not down in half an hour send up some of the bikies.'

The knock was so subtle that if I hadn't been listening for it I might have missed it altogether.

I opened the door and saw the kung fu shoes. They weren't

kung fu shoes at all but casuals made of the finest Italian leather. I liked the way they stayed flat on the floor and didn't come up to kick me in the head.

'Claudia Valentine? Joel Cairo.' The handshake lingered a little too long to be merely polite.

'If you're looking for the Maltese Falcon you've come to the wrong place.'

All this landed at his feet like a pile of wet rags. He was not unattractive but he was going to have to do something about the name. Close up he looked even better than he had at Darling Harbour. Still urbane and elegant but now I could see the eyes. They were innocent like babies' eyes but he was neither innocent nor a baby. I'd seen those eyes on tai chi masters. They came from a mind untroubled by emotion, a stilled lake that reflected but did not reveal. Also, he had the clearest skin I've ever seen on any human being over the age of ten. Not one blackhead in sight.

'Memorable name, don't you think? Your own is not entirely forgettable. Did you pick it yourself?'

'No. Like greatness, it was thrust upon me. By someone who used to be my father. Are you here to help me or am I here to help you? While you're answering, perhaps you'd better sit down.'

He sat on the floor, without even looking round to see there were no chairs. There was a bowl of fresh purple-green figs on my low lacquer table. He picked one up and felt its plumpness. Then he set it aside. I noticed a faint scar on the back of his hand.

'Eat it,' I said, sitting down cross-legged opposite him.

His eyes widened slightly and a faint smile crept to the corners of his lips.

'You play with my fruit, you don't discard it, you eat it.'

'Nothing would give me greater pleasure,' he said, his eyes not so innocent now. He popped the entire fig into his mouth. I watched his throat ripple as he swallowed. 'So succulent, and that deliciously soft yielding centre. Wouldn't you agree, Miss Valentine?'

'Since you're being so familiar with my fruit you may as well call me Claudia. And you still haven't told me why you're here.'

'I believe we may be able to help each other.'

'Yes? And what makes you think that?'

'We may hold the key to each other's problems.'

'Supposing that we do, what are you offering?'

'Six thousand years of civilisation,' he said.

It didn't count for much in Sydney.

Once again I was in Woollahra but it wasn't a corner block of flats in a narrow street and it wasn't to meet Mr Chen. It was an oriental antiques gallery in Queen Street and I was meeting the man who called himself Joel Cairo.

The young girl at the desk nodded politely and asked if she could be of help. I told her I was just looking.

So I looked. At ceramic bowls, some of them dating from a time when Europe was still full of Vikings raping and pillaging. Then at a jade statue of Kuan Yin, goddess of mercy and compassion. She was also the patron saint of tai chi, the ultimate martial art. Every statue or picture I'd ever seen of her was serene and this one was no exception.

The man who called himself Joel Cairo walked in. The young girl greeted him as if she knew him and as if she'd like to get to know him even better. When she finally released him he came over to me.

'You've been here before,' I remarked.

'Reminds me of home,' he explained, sliding over my innuendo. 'My father collects antiques.'

I thought of something Lucy had said about the Chens. About John Chen being offed just as he was about to 'go into' antiques.

'Risky business, is it?'

'Not from my father's point of view. He has a more scholarly approach.'

'Have you inherited the interest?'

'Some.'

'Look,' I said, 'before we go any further, there's no way I'm going to keep calling you Joel Cairo.'

He smiled invitingly. 'The name's Ho. James Ho.'

He handed me an ID card issued in Hong Kong.

James Ho, private investigator.

So there was another detective on my patch. I didn't know if I liked that or not. Usually I worked on my own but James Ho was interesting to say the least. I wasn't such an old dog that I couldn't learn a few new tricks.

As he took his card back I again noticed the scar on his hand.

'Old war wound?' I commented.

'A little something I picked up at the baccarat tables, from a player who didn't like losing.'

I was learning new tricks already. 'And what does his hand look like?'

'The gentleman is no longer with us,' he said smoothly. 'Shall we go on to something more interesting?'

He led me into another room, to a display of lacquer cabinets. He stopped in front of one and gazed at it.

'You see the dragons inlaid in gold on the sides?' he said. 'There are spirit dragons which rise to heaven and earthly dragons hidden in the earth which protect treasure. In the Hsia dynasty one of the kings collected the foam from the mouth of two dragons and put it in a box. For centuries no-one dared open it.'

'I know about dragon breath, I've seen *Excalibur*.'

'Yes, and King Arthur is the son of Uther Pendragon—dragon's head.'

'How very well informed you are, James.'

'I went to school in England. Got the best of both worlds.' He went on. 'In the reign of the tenth king of the Chou dynasty the box was opened and the dragon foam spread throughout the castle. It became an evil thing. Like all power it is volatile. Since that time there has been a tradition among certain noble families to place objects of power in boxes and lock them with a key. This cabinet is interesting, don't you think? See the drawers inside? Even the sides and the back which are not normally visible have been decorated. That of course is a mark of a family of great wealth. And inside again are more drawers and secret compartments, so that sometimes, even if you have the key, you can't get to the inner compartments. Boxes within boxes within boxes. Many of the boxes that you see here have become separated from each other but some sets we believe have remained intact. The Buddha boxes are the ones I'm particularly interested in.'

'Buddha boxes?'

'My father has spent his life researching them and evidence which came to light last year in Shaanxi province now proves his theory that they still exist.' He handed me some photocopied pages headed 'Rare Buddha Relics Unearthed'.

'The Buddha boxes contain fragments of fingerbones. The fingerbones of Gautama Buddha.'

I was impressed. It was like finding the Turin shroud, only better. And it hadn't yet been discredited as the shroud had.

'It's all in there,' he said, running his hand over the photocopy. 'You can read it at your leisure. Briefly, it describes the discovery of one set of boxes containing Buddha's finger.'

'So there must be nine others?'

'Oh, at least. There are also shadow bones, replicas of the real things.'

'OK, I'm impressed. But I'm sure you didn't come all the way to Sydney to tell me this.'

'No, but I think you should know it. It is believed that a set of Buddha boxes has made its way to your fair city.'

'Who has them?'

His smile was almost inscrutable. 'The matter that I am involved in is more complicated than that. It may jeopardise things if I were to reveal anything further. Besides, I am not yet sure of the exact location. But the key that you are looking for might open the boxes. It does not rightly belong to any individual, it belongs in a museum. Now, if I had a more exact description of it . . .'

He was telling me everything and he was telling me nothing.

He had six thousand years of civilisation and was willing to swap it for a description of one little key. But he wasn't going to get it. Not yet. Not till I had a few more pieces in place. It might just prove to be the pawn that could checkmate a king.

I left James Ho, private investigator, in the willing company of the young antiques lady and went back to the Daimler. I drove to a quiet spot in Centennial Park and took out the photocopy.

It had been taken from *China Reconstructs*, November 1987.

Fragments of Buddha's fingerbones had indeed been found during reconstruction work on Famen Temple in Shaanxi province. Encased in 'Eight Precious Caskets'. It gave quite a detailed description of these, from the outer one made of silver with a cover of sandalwood, to the last, made of gold and encrusted with gems. The crown jewels looked like trinkets in comparison. The relics were worshipped, by both emperors and common folk, and did the rounds of the temples. When Buddhism came under attack around 840 AD the monks were ordered to smash the relics but smashed shadow bones instead and hid away the real thing. 'Knowledge of the whereabouts of the relic was lost and 1113 years passed before it once again saw the light of day.'

I scanned the article for references to keys but found nothing. Not a lot about dragons either though they seemed to be cropping up everywhere else.

Everything else Ho had said was accruate. If there was a key that opened such boxes, where was it? If the Chens had it, how had it come to be in their possession?

It was time to make a report to the client. Or rather, for the client to make a report to me.

It was dinner time when I arrived at the Red Dragon but I hadn't come to eat.

'Table for one?' said the waiter.

'No. I've come to see Mrs Chen. Tell her it's Claudia Valentine.'

There was too much red and gold about to make me feel comfortable but it wasn't putting off the mostly Chinese clientele or the tourist parties predictably ordering sweet and sour pork and fried rice. There were wooden screens with dark red dragons and red lanterns with gold tassels. Even the waiters and waitresses wore red.

The waiter returned. He informed me that Mrs Chen was in a meeting and asked if I could come back tomorrow.

I knew all about this 'in a meeting' business.

'No, now will be just fine.'

I walked in the direction he had come from, to a steamy kitchen where chefs in sweaty singlets and aprons were slaving over hot stoves. Next to the kitchen was a set of stairs.

The waiter followed me up but I was strides ahead of him.

I came into a huge banquet room, with the same red and gold, only not so much of it. But there were no banquets in progress, only a game of cards with six players silhouetted against windows that looked over Chinatown.

I recognised Mrs Chen and I recognised someone else. He looked older than the photo on the back of his flattering 'autobiography' but he was just as smooth. Smooth as an oil slick.

Mrs Chen stopped in mid-deal at my appearance and the others followed suit. The party took on the aspect of a frieze. The only sign of animation was Mrs Chen's eyes as they moved from the cards to me.

The moment unfroze and the film reeled on.

'Care to join us, Miss Valentine?'

'Then you'd have an odd number.'

'Seven is a lucky number.'

'Not with me at the table. I would like to have a brief word with you and I think you'd prefer if it was in private.'

The waiter was hovering ineffectually in the wings.

'Huang-Tso, ask Charles to come up,' she said without turning her head or batting an eyelid.

'I would rather talk to you, Mrs Chen.'

'And who will act as banker while we have our private conversation?' Condescension oozed out of her like honey. 'Excuse me, gentlemen.'

The gentlemen excused her.

She unlocked a door marked PRIVATE and ushered me in.

The room had a low black glass table with a sofa nearby and a sideboard with ornate carving, above which was a portrait shrouded in white gauze.

'Coffee?' she asked.

'No, thank you. Tell me about the boxes.'

'The boxes? Which boxes do you mean?'

'The boxes the key opens.'

She looked mystified but her fingers tensed ever so slightly. 'The key is simply an object of sentimental value, a beautiful work of art. It is not the key to anything. It has been in our family for generations. Charles inherited it on his eighteenth birthday.'

'Shouldn't such a beautiful object belong in a museum?'

She laughed, as if the idea was simply ludicrous.

'It is ours. It is no less beautiful in a private collection than it is in a museum.'

'Maybe, but you can't have had much enjoyment from it if it was stuck away in a safety deposit box.'

She tilted back her head slightly with a haughty expression. 'Miss Valentine, it is not really your concern where we choose to keep our valuables, now is it?' The expression changed to a look that on anyone else would have been described as chummy. 'Do sit down and have a cup of coffee with me.'

'I'll stand, if you don't mind. I like the view from up here.' I leant against the sideboard, looking up at the gauze-shrouded portrait.

'My husband,' said Mrs Chen simply. 'He passed away some months ago.'

'I believe you've had more than one death in the family recently. I believe you recently lost a waiter. Ellis Wong.'

She sat up straighter and tightened her lips. 'Not what you would call family, I hardly knew the man. He worked here only casually.'

'Depends on your definition of family. I notice Mickey Doolan sits at your table. Is he "family"?'

'He was a friend of my husband.'

'He's also a smart dude.'

'Smart dude?'

'Keeps breaking the law and getting away with it. Perhaps you should ask him about your key. He could probably organise a complete line-up of bank robbers for you to choose from.'

Mrs Chen said nothing.

'Why did you hire me? Wouldn't it have been simpler to place an ad in the paper? "Lost: one gold key with dragon. Reward offered".'

Mrs Chen gave what almost passed for a laugh. 'It is a somewhat delicate matter. First, what sort of reward does one offer for an item such as this? If it is still in the hands of the bank robbers who have gained some millions of dollars, a reward of a few thousand is laughable, whereas a much larger reward would arouse suspicion. However,' she smoothed the side of her hair which was already immaculately in place, 'the key may become more visible if there is an appropriate lure. If your fee is not enough, if you need more money...'

Mrs Chen suddenly didn't look so haughty.

'More money is not going to make me do my job any better. I need information. And I need to know who I can trust. I hope it is you, Mrs Chen.'

I waited for a reply but she was as silent as the sphinx.

'Your guests must be waiting, Mrs Chen. I'll see myself out.'

There were lots of people about in Dixon Street—some going places, others just enjoying the scenery. That's all Dixon Street is nowadays—scenery. Like most of Sydney the facade of Chinatown has been sanitised, made into just another tourist attraction.

I remembered my first trip to Chinatown with my grandmother. She'd suggested I wear something light but I'd insisted on wearing my green velvet number. It was my 'best dress'. I sweltered in it all day and somehow Chinatown for me was always associated with that heat, and the characteristic smell of spices in the long dark narrow shops that your eyes had to grow accustomed to when you went in. Then, the restaurants were still seedy and people argued with the merchants. I had expected everyone to wave flags or something when my grandmother came to Chinatown. She was a hero.

Before I was born she had saved a Chinaman's life. There were market gardens where she lived and the Chinamen still wore pigtails and long coats. She had saved the Chinaman's life by telling the street kids who were beating him up to piss off. She didn't say 'piss off' though, she said 'clear off'.

Next day he came back and gave her a willow pattern plate. When Mina and I moved in with her she would often tell me the story of that plate. Both stories. How she got it and the story of the lovers. Years later I discovered that the story of the lovers was an English fabrication, not Chinese at all. I liked her story better anyway.

We always went to the same shop. The family which ran the shop was the Chinaman's family. They gave me lotus cakes and fussed over me like a doll. A tall red-haired doll.

The shop as I remembered it was no longer there. There weren't any of those shops now. They were mini supermarkets and well-lit. That Chinatown I knew as a child had disappeared. It had gone underground. Or high above ground. On first floors of restaurants where owners played cards with the elite of the underworld.

I took the lift up to the seventh floor of the Remington Building in Oxford Street. There was no security, no-one stopped me, not even the uniformed cop who shared the life with me, at least to the second floor.

'I've got a machine-gun in my handbag and a couple of canisters of tear-gas,' I said as he got out. The doors had closed before I caught his reply.

Even on the seventh floor, where Carol had told me I'd find Jim Campbell, no-one was overly interested in my appearance.

I found him eventually, one of the big boys in the Breaking Squad. And they were all big boys. No-one under six foot tall or weighing less than sixteen stone.

The Breaking Squad headquarters was a large sparse office with grey metal filing cabinets and five desks—one for each of the detectives.

'Things seem pretty quiet around here,' I said to Campbell when he offered me a seat.

'That's just the way we like it.'

The only police business that seemed to be going on was Campbell getting out the folder of Haymarket Bank Robbery photos to show me. All the other 'boys' were gathered around one desk—two sitting on chairs and one sitting on the desk swivelling a chair with his foot. Despite the signs with the familiar red circle with a diagonal red line across a lit cigarette, one of the boys was smoking.

Before Campbell could open the folder his phone rang. My ears were listening to two different conversations. Campbell wasn't giving much away but tickets for the cricket were mentioned. My other ear was listening to the weighty detective sitting on the desk across the way. He was giving the others details of a fruit diet he was trying. Today was day four and for lunch he'd had eight bananas. On Thursday he'd be having soup and on Friday, brown rice. 'I suppose you put what's left of the soup on the brown rice,' said one of those seated on a chair. He wasn't joking. In fact they were all listening to the guy on the desk as if he were a boxing coach instructing his fighters on some fine tactical points. Things had changed in the Police Force. Though there still weren't any women in the Breaking Squad.

Campbell had arranged his tickets and the time he'd be meeting the person who'd placed the call.

He got down to business.

The folder held a set of colour photos, much clearer and more detailed than any of the newspaper ones. They were arranged in an order that traced the footsteps of the breakers, and though they lacked human subjects you could see where the breakers had been. The photos started with several views of the scaffolding, the open first floor windows and, lo and behold, a print in the dusty boards of the scaffolding of a size nine running-shoe. The sort of thing you read about in Sherlock Holmes. The series ended with shots of a variety of safety deposit boxes.

Along the way there were details that hadn't made it to the papers and Campbell threw in some background facts.

The bank occupied one side of the ground floor of the building. On higher floors were offices—lawyers, an optometrist, and other professional people.

The building also had a basement, accessible by the lift, but only if you had a key. And only the bank had a key.

Not a lot of people knew that down in the basement were strong-rooms and millions of dollars. But the breakers knew. They also knew about lift circuitry because they'd wired the lift to access the basement. Evidence of this was in the photo of the roof of the lift, along with about two hundred feet of green garden hose and numerous detonators, or 'dets' as Campbell described them. The hose was used to stream water for the blasting. So the money wouldn't burn.

There was a photo similar to one I'd seen in the newspapers of the blasted-off lock to the first grilled security door that led to the strong-room area. It was when the breakers tried the strong-room door that they set off an alarm that was vibration-sensitive—you didn't need to blast it, all you had to do was hit it with a hammer.

The patrolling security guard got the call and went to investigate the bank. He looked at the safe on the ground floor and found it in pristine condition. He probably shrugged his shoulders and went away. Anyone who lives in Sydney knows that there are many false or at least faulty alarms. They go off all the time disturbing the peace till someone gets out of bed and turns them off. The guard probably didn't even know there was another safe in the basement.

Meanwhile the breakers worked on. It was heavy work. They were lucky, and they were unlucky. They were lucky the guard didn't find them—lucky twice. An alarm had gone off a second time and a second guard had come to investigate. This one had gone into the basement, seen the cardboard cartons the breakers had piled up in front of the security door and had gone away thinking it was just a storage area. The breakers may have been only two feet away from him, holding their breath, hoping the guard didn't have a dog that could smell their surging adrenalin.

The steel door wasn't yielding so they blasted a hole in the three-foot-thick brick wall. The door wasn't yielding because it was coated with a substance that made it fireproof. The oxy-welding flame just slid down it.

The blast to the brick wall could have been heard from the street but there were lots of other explosions that night. New Year's Eve. An extra special New Year, the start of the Bicentennial. Next day it would be 1988 and the white folk were kicking up their heels. Celebrating two hundred years of what passes for civilisation in the antipodes.

There was a photo of the hole in the wall and the next one was of a fist-sized hole in the top of a safe. It looked like a cankerous sore. The breakers had put silastic round the seams of the safe door and filled it up with water from the hose now immortalised on the roof of the lift. But the force of the blast had flung the silastic out and blown the money and the documents to smithereens. This is what Campbell called unlucky. The money had shredded and the next photo showed bits of it stuck to the walls. I wondered if the breakers had said something stronger than 'blast!' when that had happened. They had tried the same thing on the second safe but had abandoned it. But they weren't, after all that, going to go away empty-handed.

They came to the boxes, one of which held the Chens' key. They were in cupboards with sliding doors, unlocked. Going through the boxes took time but it was easy work. No blasting, no alarms. All they had to do was flick off the padlocks with a screwdriver. They went through eighty of them. The photo showed about fifteen metal boxes of different sizes. Some were ordinary anodised metal tool boxes while others were old-fashioned tin boxes with brass hinges. This surprised me. I thought they would all be regulation bank issue. 'No,' said Campbell, 'they bring their own boxes in, already padlocked.' The boxes had numbers on them and only the bank had the list of names that corresponded to the numbers. 'And,' said Campbell, 'they wouldn't give the list to us.' I already knew this from Carol, and knew how much it gave the police the shits to have their hands tied by 'legalities'. No padded leather chair would entice me into the Force.

'What we do know is that they were all old established Chinatown customers. They've been using this bank for years. It's traditional. Look at that box, it's bloody antique.'

The word 'antique', like the dragon, was coming up a bit too frequently for my liking.

'Are the Chinese doing anything about it themselves?'

Campbell shrugged. 'Who knows? If they are they're not telling us. They don't usually come to the police with their problems. That's also traditional.'

'You think Triads are involved?'

'Not in the break-in; they don't need to do that to extort money from Chinatown. Whoever's been running the rackets down there has been doing a pretty good job. Things have been quiet in Chinatown for years; everyone pays their dues and no-one gets their business torched. But the last few months things have changed. We don't get the full picture but from the bits and pieces that come our way I'd say someone's trying to move in. People with no respect for "tradition",' he said disparagingly. 'Take this Ellis Wong case,' he said, leaning his brawny arms on the desk. 'What you've got is organised gangs of Viets standing over the Chinese businessmen. They go into a restaurant in Cabramatta or Chinatown and mock up a fight, break a few windows. Then they say to the guy that for five hundred a week they can protect the restaurant from further damage. If they don't pay up there'll be a fight in there every Saturday night. Now customers don't like that sort of thing and tend to stay away. No customers, no business. So the guy pays the five hundred. Then he goes and sees the bloke he's already paying dues to and complains that he's not getting his protection. Once or twice they've come to us but it never gets to court. They don't want trouble. And you try and talk to witnesses and they've all gone suddenly deaf, dumb and blind. Unlike the people dobbing in the bank breakers.'

My heart did a quiet somersault. 'You know who did it?'

'I know the people who think they know the people. About nine thousand so far.'

'Oh.' My heart settled back into place.

'And,' he said, wearily stretching out his legs and putting his hands behind his head, 'we've investigated each and every one, and each and every one has gone nowhere fast.'

'Got any private ideas, detective?'

'No more than the average punter. Could have been anybody.'

No, not anybody. It was people who knew about oxy-welding, explosives and lift circuitry and who'd managed to get hold of the necessary equipment. They were strong and fit enough to carry that equipment in, they were smart and they'd done their homework. And one of them wore size nine running-shoes. Now what would it take to flush out people like that?

'The photos were great. Thanks for your time,' I said as I got up to go.

'If you hear anything you will let us know.' It was a statement more than a request.

I smiled a Chen smile. 'Give my regards to Detective Rawlins.'

'I will,' he said. 'Tomorrow, in fact. She's taking me to the cricket.'

As I walked towards the door Campbell's phone started ringing.

'Hey!'

I turned around. He beckoned me back. It wasn't a friendly gesture.

'Where's your handbag?' he said, with a certain amount of intimidation.

'I don't have one with me.'

The other cops approached and surrounded me.

'What's this all about?' I asked.

He ignored me. 'Turn out your pockets.'

I sighed, but obliged.

I placed on his desk my car keys, ID, a pen and some paper, sunglasses and a tube of Red Haze lipstick.

'Everyone happy?' I enquired. 'Now what's going on?'

'Just received a report that a woman answering your description is running round the building with canisters of tear-gas.'

'I think someone's pulling your leg, Sergeant. Good day.'

Steve said why not his place—Collier always looked like he could do with a home-cooked meal. You wouldn't exactly describe Collier as thin and undernourished, it was more the fact that he ate out a lot.

When I had people to dinner I usually took them to the pub restaurant. My living quarters weren't really set up for entertaining, though sometimes I entertained Steve in my room with Jack acting as room service. He did this on special occasions. If I got ahead in the pool stakes we sometimes cleared the slate with Jack's room service. Steve liked it too, said it made him feel like he was away on a dirty weekend.

So we were having dinner at Steve's and Collier was going to get as home-cooked as they come. Steak and kidney pie and a mountain of potatoes.

Steve went to answer the door while I tore up lettuce leaves and made a vinaigrette. Not exactly traditional Aussie tucker but at least it didn't have balsamic vinegar in it. I heard the door open then jocular tones of men greeting each other.

As they came into the loungeroom Steve asked Brian what he'd like to drink. He'd like a Scotch if we had it.

'Evening Brian,' I said, taking my chef's drink into the lounge, 'how're things in the real world?'

'Business as usual.' He looked around the room approvingly but didn't say 'nice place you've got here'. Brian had made an effort for tonight. His hair had been slicked back with water and there was a faint odour in the room that suggested aftershave. I didn't particularly go for it. Unlike the women in the ads I found it easy to resist. I liked men to smell like men. Up close, in the warm areas like armpits and the crook of the elbow, Steve smelled like newly-baked bread. Good enough to eat.

I didn't feel all that comfortable with the situation. Though it was Steve's idea to do it here, I was entertaining a guest in someone else's home. Besides, my reasons for inviting Brian to dinner weren't strictly philanthropic.

I served the pie, potatoes and huge bowl of salad greens.

'I want to put an ad in the paper,' I said, as Brian tucked into his second helping of potatoes.

He wiped his mouth with the serviette, moving a bit of potato over to his cheek. I tried not to stare at it.

'Lost and found, is it?'

'Don't know. More like lonely hearts. Looking for someone who wears a size nine shoe, shows initiative, sense of adventure, an oxy-welder or maybe an electrician, maybe someone who works, sorry, worked in a bank, willing to give me the key to his heart.'

'Well that should narrow it down to a few million. What about the Wednesday Meeting Place? You'd be surprised who reads that. What are you offering a man with twenty million dollars?'

'Not money. Something he couldn't possibly resist.'

Steve and Brian began to take a real interest in the conversation.

'What is it that a man can't resist?' asked Steve, rubbing his leg against mine under the table. I moved my leg away, but not immediately.

'I'm open to suggestions,' I said.

'Couple of tickets to Hong Kong?' asked Steve. 'What do you reckon, Brian?'

Brian laid his knife and fork carefully side by side, and lit the cigarette he'd been dying to have all evening.

'The chance to have been Mr Christian,' he said, leaning back and exhaling slowly. 'Lead a mutiny and start a new colony on some idyllic South Sea island.'

'It wasn't idyllic where they ended up,' I said.

'It would be in my version.'

I didn't know a lot of people in the underworld and that was the way I liked it. I had my networks but they were mostly clean, only touching on the raggy edges. But occasionally I needed a man like Mickey Doolan. Or his henchmen. I knew people who knew people and Collier was one of them.

'There's something else I'd like you to help me with,' I said to Brian while Steve was getting the port. 'I'd like to meet a few people who think they might know something about this matter, people who wouldn't necessarily be Meeting Place readers, the sort of people who would feel comfortable in a pub like the Painters and Dockers in Rozelle. I'll be there the night after next should anyone like a discreet little chat. Someone must know something they're not telling the cops.'

'Yeah? And what do I tell the sleazebags?'

'You're good at stories, you'll think of something. Tell them I'm writing a book about it or something. Discretion guaranteed, of course. I mean, all it is is one little key.'

'For one little key it sounds like one lot of trouble.'

The more I thought about the bank job the more I found myself admiring the minds behind it.

'Don't worry about it. Everybody does,' said Steve on the edge of sleep. 'What about Ronnie Biggs? He became not only a local but an international hero. The ones who buck the system, even if it is for only a while. That's the stuff Hollywood dreams are made of. And even you are not immune.' He kissed me lightly between my breasts. 'G'night, Magnum.'

I was starting to fall asleep, close enough to Steve to feel his body heat but not touching. 'Carol thinks I'm going to round them up,' I said drowsily.

In the dark Steve chuckled. I could feel the ripples. The air stirred slightly and brushed the sheet against our bodies.

Before I finally sank to the depths of sleep an image flickered into view. It was of James Ho eating my fig. The feeling it gave me was not entirely unpleasurable.

It was 3 a.m. and I was sitting in Steve's bath composing an ad. The doors were open and thin moonlight defined the edges of the jungle in the courtyard. There was probably more oxygen in those four square metres than in the rest of Newtown combined. Two cat's eyes flashed as the animal prowled by intent on doing whatever it is cats do who are up and prowling in the small hours. It wasn't even garbage night.

You see different sorts of things when the city is supposed to be sleeping. And think different thoughts.

There were people out there in the sleeping city who knew who had done the bank job. Three people at least.

I imagined, as I'd imagined when looking at the photographs and reading the newspaper reports, that I was there with them. And I imagined the days before the job, the discussions they must have had, the planning. It may have started out as a wild idea over dinner, or after a game of squash. In the pub after a few quiet beers. And the plan had been formulated. A list of equipment drawn up? No. Nothing on paper. Sussing out the bank, casing the joint. One of them may have been familiar with it. To know that unlike safety deposit boxes in other banks which usually held only important documents, these ones held treasure. And the layout? You could always get a detailed plan of the building. All you had to do was dress like an architect and ask the council for it. And the night? Of course that night was ideal. Even more so than any other New Year's Eve. The eve of the Bicentennial. Starting it off with a bang.

I went through it all, putting myself in those size nine shoes. Went through it step by step as the photos had shown it. Weeks later now and the cops had no leads. No-one had come knocking on my door. I'd pulled it off. No hitches. Twenty million dollars and a lot of trinkets richer.

What were they doing now? Sleeping soundly in suburbia on a mattress of money? Or were they awake like me, thinking about it?

I closed my eyes. The water was cold but I hardly noticed. I was thinking about them. Now. A month after the job.

A month after the job and the trail dead. Nothing in the

newspapers, nothing anywhere. No-one else knew a thing. The biggest job in Australia's history and no-one knew.

And that was the trouble. No-one knew. The event had been anonymous. You'd pulled off the greatest robbery in Australian history and no-one knew that it was you who had carefully planned and executed it, carried it through. Wouldn't you want to shout out: 'That was me, that was my work, my brainchild!' If you knew you would be safe, it there was an absolute guarantee that you would not be prosecuted for speaking, you'd get up on top of the Harbour Bridge with a megaphone and shout it to the whole city.

It might even be enough, just enough, to whisper it to one person in private.

As I pulled out the plug I began composing the ad. It was the first week of February. I now had a date picked out—the fourteenth. I would place it with the Valentine messages.

When I'd asked Lucy to tell me more about the Chens she'd directed me to her father. 'He did welfare work in Chinatown for years. Still goes down there a couple of times a week. He'll probably tell you all you want to know and more about Chinatown. But Claudia, do it discreetly, hey?'

We met at the Swan Cafe at the corner of Goulburn and Dixon Streets. There used to be a service station here before sanitisation. A drunk had been found dead outside it for no apparent reason. In those days I checked out all the dead deroes to see whether one of them was my father. That was in the days before I became a private investigator, but looking in garbage had stood me in good stead. So had going to university.

There was a dark green pagoda structure in front of the cafe that looked a bit like a bus-stop. You went up a few stairs to sit in the cafe, either on the terrace or inside. It looked like an Italian espresso bar but as well as coffee they served things like sweet almond milk. There were young Chinese men sitting outside and some mums with crawling babies.

Mr Lau wanted to sit inside. People in the cafe said hello to him. He was clean-shaven and neatly dressed in a shirt and tie. He looked too young to be Lucy's father.

Lucy introduced us fairly formally. It wasn't her usual style.

'You will stay, Lucy?'

It was a question of faint hope.

'For a while, Dad. I have to get back to work.'

She slid into the bench opposite and we ordered coffees.

'Lucy tells me you are interested in the history of the Chinese in Australia.'

'Well actually...' I felt Lucy kick me under the table '... yes, I am.'

He launched into what appeared to be one of his favourite subjects.

'I have done welfare work in Chinatown for thirty years. In the early days my family had an import–export business here but not any longer. The building was demolished a few years ago to make way for the new property development. I do not regret it; we got a good price for it. Good enough to put my children through university.'

Lucy rolled her eyes a little and I brought the conversation back to things less personal.

At the end of an hour I had not only the story of the Lau family but a rather panoramic history of the Chinese in Australia.

The first Chinese in Australia settled in the Rocks in the 1830s then moved to the Haymarket when real estate got too expensive. And talking about real estate, the famous L. J. Hooker was Chinese. His given name was Tin You. In the early days there were 8000 men to one woman. The Chinese could bring out their menfolk as labourers but they had to be property owners before they could bring out women. Owning property also made a man a better marriage prospect back in China. So the brides who came out were often better educated and from higher social classes than their husbands. As a consequence they became influential members of the new community. They still were.

There were political divisions and religious divisions. When the Chinese arrived in Sydney they went to where their clan was and only did business with people from their own village. Now nobody cared about this, said Mr Lau, only those keepers of tradition—the old ladies. The joss houses were associated with clans as well. The Ko You one in Alexandria and the Sze Yap in Glebe.

Once, there had been many opium dens and gambling houses. Fantan. Mr Lau was proud to have been one of the Chinese who had helped clean up Chinatown. As an influential Chinese man the police had asked him how this might be done. Of course a white face wouldn't have a chance of getting in through the door. But the door wasn't the only way. There were also the roofs. The Fire Brigade got their ladders up there and busted the joints. And that, as far as Mr Lau was concerned, was the end of it.

Lucy looked as if she'd heard this story many times. She had to go.

'You will ring your mother, won't you.'

'Bye Dad,' she said in a strained voice, 'bye Claudia.'

'My third daughter has moved away from our community,' he said rather sadly. 'She is more Australian. But that is the way of things. That is progress. I have liberal views. I gave my daughters the same opportunities as my sons. I belong to many associations. I want what's best for our children and our community.'

'Does Victoria Chen also want what's best for the community?'

'Mrs Chen is on many committees.' He reeled off a list of what sounded like high society charities. 'I sometimes meet Mrs Chen at one association or another but I also concern myself with the poor. Chinese people are envious of the good fortune of others. It is not good to have others envy your success. If you are in a position to help those less fortunate than yourself you have a social obligation to do so. For the good of the community.'

'How did the community feel about the robbery at the National Bank?'

'They did not care much,' he said, without batting an eyelid. 'Those who lost valuables were mainly newcomers from Hong Kong. They do not care about the community. Mainly they invest outside Chinatown, to allay envy.'

Campbell had said it was the traditional banking spot, and I'd seen the photos of old, well-worn safety deposit boxes. They didn't look like the boxes of newcomers. Now seemed like a good opportunity to turn the conversation to Triads.

'A good media story,' he said, laughing. 'It is nothing. There are some gangs of youths who come into a restaurant and say they are going to make trouble if you don't pay them money. They show you the dragon tattoo on their arm and say they will tell Big Brother if you do not pay. You ask them to take you to Big Brother and they can't. Because Big Brother doesn't exist! The gangs are just naughty boys, they belong to no organisation.'

All afternoon he'd been telling me about associations, clans and communities. I'd bet my bottom dollar crime wasn't going to be left out of that sort of structure. More than half the heroin in Australia came in through Chinatown. This was more than naughty boys.

'Why the dragon tattoo?'

'It is the throne, the emperor.'

Big Brother.

The sun was setting behind the Swan Cafe and it was time to go.

'I have some books here,' he said, delving into a briefcase. 'They will perhaps be of help for your research project.'

So that's what Lucy had told him, that I was doing research. Well in a way I was. It never ceased to amaze me how malleable was the bright rod of Truth.

Which was just as well. Because everyone I talked to about Chinatown had a different story to tell.

The painters and Dockers pub in Rozelle was a rose by another name but everyone called it the Painters and Dockers. Because of the clientele.

I ordered a mineral water and put the change into the juke-box. The records hadn't been changed in fifteen years. Joplin started belting out *Piece of My Heart*. She sounded like she was trying too hard.

It wasn't a pub I was particularly fond of—they watered down their spirits and never emptied the ashtrays. All the drinkers seemed to know each other and conversation would stop when a newcomer, especially a woman, entered. There were only one or two women among the locals, their faces wrinkled from a lifetime of beer and cigarettes. When I started chatting to the barman as if I knew him conversation started up again. I did know him, vaguely. I'd met him once or twice through Jack. Jack wasn't overly fond of Dennis and without seeking out his company maintained the wary friendship of fellow traders. They had their separate niches in the trade, with different clientele. It was in this pub seven years ago that Mickey Doolan had shot a man dead and bought off all the witnesses. No-one testified against him. So it seemed an ideal rendezvous for me and the underworld.

Besides, I didn't want to shit in my own nest.

Sitting there looking at every man who walked in and some who were already there, I felt like a hooker sizing up potential. I decided no amount of money would entice me into that ancient profession, even though you did get to keep your own hours.

I'd told Brian to use my surname when he passed the message along. They could remain anonymous but as a gesture of sincerity they could have that much.

The first guy stood next to me, leaning on the bar.

'Valentine,' he said, looking straight ahead at the shelves of bottles.

'Sorry mate,' said the barman, 'no cocktails.'

The guy mumbled something, then more audibly said, 'Give us a schooner of new then.'

'I could possibly fix you up,' I said.

He turned and looked at me. He was fairly neatly dressed for someone who looked like he'd just come out of jail.

'You wanna know about that bank job?'

His subtlety knew no bounds.

'I coulda done that, I'd been planning it. That was gunna be me next job once I got out. Those bastards beat me to it.'

'Which bastards?'

'Bastards,' he said softly, more to himself. 'It was no great shakes, I coulda done it. All you needed was a good bit of gelly. I'd staked that joint out before I went inside the last time. I was gunna do that then retire.'

'They were pretty smart bastards. Lot of planning went into that job. Who would you have on your team?'

'They weren't so smart, anyone coulda done it. It would have been easy blowin' that safe. And I wouldn't have needed fellas to help me, I woulda done it on me own.'

I was getting nowhere fast with this one.

'Do you know how they did it, these bastards?'

'Read about it in the papers. Like taking candy from a baby. Bastards.'

His conversation had a circular quality and no matter how I varied the questions the answers were all the same. He wasn't there to give me information, he was there to peel some sour grapes.

Unfortunately the pub turned out to be full of men like him. As the night wore on a few more sidled up to me—people who really didn't have a clue but who rankled with professional jealousy. I had a few enquiries as to what a nice girl like me was doing in a place like this to which I replied that I didn't come here often. Things weren't looking good.

'Ms Valentine?'

I swivelled around. It was Detectives Campbell and Rawlins.

'Enjoy the cricket?'

'It was business,' said Carol, not looking all that comfortable, 'like tonight is.'

'Is it business that precludes drinking?' I asked, offering.

'A dry martini,' said Carol, emphasising the 'dry'.

'They don't do cocktails here.'

'A glass of white wine then.'

'Same for me,' said Campbell. 'Got to watch the weight.'

The weight wasn't the only thing he was watching; he was also scanning the room. Satisfied, he turned his attention back to us.

'Shall we sit at a table?'

'I was sitting here at the bar for a particular reason but now that I have company I don't think I'll be getting any more offers.'

'A shame,' said Carol, 'because it was those offers we were interested in.'

'News travels fast,' I said in a tone as dry as the martini Carol wasn't having. 'What brings you out of your nice big office?'

'Just thought we'd come along and see how things were progressing.'

'So now you've seen. Want to go to the toilet, Carol?'

'Not particularly.'

'Want to come and watch me?' I said more pointedly.

'Scuse us, Jim,' she said as we stood up.

I opened the door that said Ladies. It was a grotty tile job, the tap in the basin didn't work and there was no paper.

'You don't seem very pleased to see us,' said Carol.

'Well what do you think? You and your mate there stand out like the Salvation Army at an orgy.'

'And you want to have this little orgy all on your own, do you?' She became more urbane. 'We just wanted to scan the guest list. Never know what an invitation like this might bring out of the woodwork.'

'Did you think they were just going to walk in here and slip their wrists into your handcuffs? The party's over now, Carol. No-one's going to be asking me to dance now that you're here.'

'Are you going to go to the toilet?'

'In here? You're joking.'

'You've been in worse places.'

'Not for a while, Carol. How are these guys going to trust me if I bring along the uniformed brigade?'

'We're not in uniform.'

'You don't have to be. These guys can smell a cop a mile off.'

'My aftershave?' said Carol sarcastically.

'Your big feet. That you're always putting in things.'

'OK, Claudia, that's enough of the smart cracks. We only came for a look.'

'At them or me?'

'Should we be watching you, Claudia?'

'C'mon, let's get back to your mate. Can't leave the boy unprotected, can we?'

Campbell had ordered another round of drinks which sat on the table like so much extra time.

'Enjoying yourself?' I asked him.

'Not bad, not bad at all.'

I wondered how he'd feel if I turned up unexpectedly at a verbal.

'Well keep enjoying. I'm going.'

'What about your drink?' asked Campbell.

'I didn't ask for it.'

I was glad to get out into the polluted night air, it was better than the polluted air in the pub. I liked being alone; that's how I handled things best. I hadn't been getting any results but at least people were talking to me. It wasn't like Carol to inch in on me like that. She'd been persuaded. And persuading Carol was no easy feat.

These thoughts surrounded me like a little fog as I walked the dark streets towards home.

'How was it?' A voice sliced the fog like a knife through

butter. James Ho. In his immaculate suit and Italian leather casuals. I hadn't even smelled him.

'Don't you have a home to go to?'

I was fed up with people wanting to know how my business was going.

'I am far from my home while you are near yours. I thought you might invite me in for a cup of tea. Or a fig.'

'Let me tell you something. I don't appreciate being followed and I especially don't appreciate it when it takes place on my home ground. What are you doing here?'

'I'm here for the waters,' he said, a faint smile in the shadows of his face.

'The harbour's that way,' I said, pointing down the street from which he'd emerged. 'High faecal count but you might enjoy the company.'

'I would prefer yours,' he said calmly.

I walked on. And so did he. Two paces behind. I stopped. Very still. So did he. I did not turn around but I knew exactly where he was. Directly behind me. Neither tilted to the right nor to the left. He was not visible from the corner of my eye. OK, Mr James Ho, private investigator, let's see if those shoes are more than just decoration. I imagined myself in a column of impenetrable light. I moved slightly forward and with my weight on the front foot turned and kicked.

His right forearm was already there to block it and his left hand was a fist moving fast forward into a body punch. With both hands I grabbed his wrist and twisted it over, followed through by pulling the arm across the body, forcing him to turn. I pulled him into a sweep and in two seconds he was on the ground.

And he was laughing! Lying on the ground like he was relaxing beside the pool, and laughing.

Ho, bloody ho.

The bastard had been playing me. His first blocking tactic was quick and had meant business but after that he hadn't fought back, he'd just gone along for the ride. He'd yielded completely, and in yielding had won. He'd made a fool of me.

Made me feel like a little terrier yapping at an Alsatian. Old dog learning new tricks, sure. I felt frustrated and on the verge of screaming.

A white Subaru cruised alongside us. It came to a silent halt and I waited for more of Ho's mates to come flying out of it. The window on the passenger's side slid down electronically.

'Are you winning, Claudia?'

It was Carol. In a car driven by Campbell. She and Campbell got out of the car and Ho got up off the ground, never a safe place to rest in the streets of Balmain. But he didn't have any dog shit on him, he looked like he'd just stepped out of the display window at David Jones.

'This bloke bothering you?' asked Campbell, just itching for an arrest. It had been an unproductive night all round.

'Just someone I ran into.'

'There were a couple of blokes looking for you back there. You should have stayed. Could have been interesting.'

'Did you find it interesting?'

'About as interesting as all the others. All theory and no fact.'

'So you spoke to them in my stead,' I said fuming.

'Seemed a shame to pass up the opportunity,' he said smugly.

'Carol,' I said through my teeth, 'keep your boys off my patch, OK?'

'Just trying to help.'

'How can I make discreet enquiries with you two breathing down my neck? You three,' I said, including Ho. I turned to where he'd been standing but he had disappeared. Obviously he didn't want to talk to the cops any more than I wanted him to talk to them.

'So what's the word on Chinaboy?' asked Campbell.

'No word,' I said tight-lipped.

'C'mon, you can do better than that. You scratch our back, we'll scratch yours.'

The thought of Campbell scratching my back, even touching it, made my blood run cold. Beneath the wave of words was a nasty undertow, a bullying quality of a man who, when sweetness and light failed, threatened menace. Maybe that worked with break and enters but it sure wasn't the way to win my heart.

'Goodnight,' I said, 'it hasn't been a pleasure.' And walked away.

'Claudia!' It was Carol. I stopped momentarily but didn't turn around. She was having words with Campbell and they weren't nice. I heard the car door slam and started walking.

'Claudia!'

I kept walking. I could hear the rapid clack of footsteps behind me, then Carol drew level.

'He can be an arsehole, OK? I'm sorry.'

I was too fed up to be impressed with the apology, even though I knew Carol must have just about gagged on her pride to give it.

'You were there too,' I pointed out.

'Look, it didn't turn out the way we thought it would. It was strictly observation.'

'Why didn't you keep it that way, instead of making contact with me?'

'Campbell got word that someone was asking volunteers to come forward, so we came for a look. We didn't know you were the one doing the asking.'

'You must have had a fair idea.'

'You could have kept me informed, Claudia.'

'Ah, so that's what it's all about. I don't work for you, Carol. I'm not on your leash.'

Carol grimaced. She wasn't overly fond of dogs. 'But we did agree to give you full co-operation on this one. Co-operation goes both ways. *Co-operation*,' she repeated, emphasising both parts of the word.

'OK,' I said in a voice that called a truce, 'if I get any information I'll let you know. But let me go about getting it in my own way. Talking about information, did you check out that guy in the pool hall in Cabramatta?'

'Checked all of them. Nobody knows anyone and no-one's seen anything.'

'You coming in?' I asked as the bright lights of the pub came into view.

'No, it's been a long day, I haven't been home yet.'

'I'll give you a call,' I said as we came to the pub door. The pub was closing and people pushed past us to get out.

'Sure thing.' Carol lowered her voice a little. 'Claudia, just between the two of us, who was that bloke in the street?'

'A karate expert. You know, like Inspector Clouseau has. I get him to jump me in unexpected places. To keep my hand in.'

She almost believed me.

It was a relief to get home, even though I wasn't quite yet in the inner sanctum.

'Give us a Scotch, Jack.'

'Wait till I get rid of this mob then we can have a quiet drink and you can tell me what that Chinese fella was doing here again.'

'What!'

'Ten past twelve, gentlemen. Please!' said Jack.

A few more drinkers dawdled away. Jack started putting the chairs up, which entailed getting a few bums off them first.

'It's past closing time, lads.'

I gave him a hand with the chairs and Jack started locking the doors. George, our local fixture, was the hardest to shift. Not that he became stroppy, he just got more friendly and would point out, as he did every night, how long he'd been a customer.

'C'mon, George, we'll still be here tomorrow.' Jack put his arm around George and in this intimate fashion was able to steer him to the one remaining open door. When George finally tumbled out Jack locked it.

The pub was a different place with no customers.

'Want a game, Jack?'

'Sure. Set 'em up. I'll get the drinks.'

I placed the balls in the triangle and took out a two dollar coin.

'Queens or Aborigines?' I called out, tossing the coin.

'Queens,' came Jack's voice from the bar.

'You break,' I said, as Jack came into the pool-room with two

Scotches, a clean ashtray and a cigarette in his mouth. He was trying to give up smoking but pool was his critical point.

He placed the ashtray on a nearby table, selected his favourite cue, ground its tip into the blue chalk and took aim. He pocketed a big one on the break, took a drag on the cigarette and missed the next one, but left the white ball in a difficult position.

'Thanks a lot. What did the Chinese guy want?'

'A vodka martini, shaken not stirred.'

'Oh really?' I pocketed the yellow.

'Really. Gave me quite precise instructions on how to make it. Three measures of Gordon's, one of vodka, and half a measure of something I've never heard of. Shake it until it's ice-cold, then add a large thin slice of lemon.'

'And did you?'

'I made it the way I always make it. If he noticed any difference he didn't say anything.'

I walked around the table and lined up my next shot, going for the purple.

'He left before closing time. Wish they were all as easy as that.'

'He's not so easy,' I muttered.

'I was talking about the shot.'

I missed the orange. Jack stubbed out his cigarette, bending it at a right angle in the ashtray.

'What was he doing here? Did you have a date?'

Under other circumstances a date with James Ho would be a not unattractive proposition.

'Maybe he just likes your pub,' I suggested. 'I was down at Dennis's tonight.'

'Oh yeah?' said Jack, on guard. 'What was that like?' He finished the question with yet another pocketed ball. He was doing well. Would probably clean me up.

I liked this time of night, the crowds almost still present, but the only sounds our voices punctuated by the sound of cue on ball, the slight whirr of the ceiling fan circulating stale cigarette smoke. It was no man's land, it was home. It was the time Jack and I played pool and told each other stories of our lives.

'Full of cops and would-be robbers.'

'Must have suited you down to the ground.'

'You'd think so, wouldn't you.'

Jack won the game and I declined his offer of another. In our running score we were now even. It seemed appropriate to leave it at that for tonight.

'No, not for me,' I said as Jack poured another Scotch. 'I'm going to lie down for a few hours. 'Night.' And I climbed the stairs to my room.

I felt the heat as soon as I opened the door, an almost palpable presence. I turned the light on in the kitchen just in time to see a large Balmain cockroach scurry away to safety. I poured myself a large glass of iced water and went to go out on the balcony.

But there was something stopping the french doors. I looked down through the upper glass part and saw what it was.

A body. Propped up against the door like a Mexican having a siesta. But it wasn't Mexican, it was Chinese.

I pushed hard at the door and the body slipped away a little. Then it stood up. With a smile on its face.

'What took you so long?' he asked.

Cold hard anger set in. The street was bad enough but finding him here on the balcony, on *my* balcony, was way out of the range of acceptability.

'I have a present for you.'

'I don't care if you have the Taj Mahal in your back pocket, you're gone, mate. Break and enter.'

'I didn't break into your premises nor have I entered them. Anyway, I have a key.' He opened his fist and there lay a key. A gold key with a dragon curled round it, like the serpent twined round the sword of Aesculapius.

'Perhaps you'd better come in. Brush the dirt off your trousers.'

'If I'm going to get dirty I don't wear trousers,' he said, suggestively raising an eyebrow.

The eyebrow quickly came back into place when he saw I wasn't in the mood for that kind of suggestion.

He came in and again sat on the floor. But this time he didn't play with my fruit, he played with the key.

'Why have you brought that here?' I asked suspiciously.

'It's yours.'

'I don't think so.'

'The key you are looking for.'

'I still don't think so. The key I'm looking for would not be so easy to find. And why would you be giving it to me anyway? Isn't it part of the set you're after?'

He looked at me with those calm eyes and smiled. 'Are you always so mistrusting, my dear Ms Valentine? Would you not accept it as a gesture of friendship, like the two dragons in the Chinese Gardens? A friend like me might prove to be helpful. You must believe, I mean you no harm.'

Trusting a smooth-talking bastard was a bit like dipping your hand in a piranha pool. But if you were careful, if you kept your armour on, maybe you could swim in the pool without even getting a nip.

'Let's assume for the moment that I believe your intentions are honourable. What about proving your trustworthiness by telling me what you might be getting out of this little venture.

'Let's say I'm using it to move things along. It looks enough like the real key to fool anyone who hasn't seen it before.'

It was similar, but not the Chens' key. A winged dragon this time, and no intricate six-toothed locking mechanism.

'But Mrs Chen would pick it straight away.'

'She would, but others might not.'

'Others?'

'It may prove a useful bargaining point.' He stood up to leave. 'Come to yum cha with me at the Red Dragon next Sunday, bring your friends, it is a time for families. You may learn something interesting. Don't bother to see me out. I know the way.'

He placed one hand on the balcony rail and jumped into the night.

The iceblocks in the water had melted away without me touching a drop. The night was still warm and carried the scent of geraniums. An eventful night but the events had no pattern to them. My attempt to sift through straws to get to the key had been thwarted by the heavy hand of the law. Then the key, or a key, had turned up. In the hands of James Ho. Not the key I was after but what had he said? A useful bargaining point? For whom? He was persistent but not menacing. I thought if I had to pick sides I'd rather be working with him than someone like Campbell.

There were no drain-pipes leading up to my balcony for a budding Romeo to climb. There was nothing but brick. He must have run up the wall. I'd seen that once, in a martial arts demonstration. With training you could run up walls.

The obvious thing, of course, was that the false key was a part of his jigsaw not mine. Somehow he needed me. And maybe I needed him. I needed someone I could trust and he was the best of a bad bunch. I wasn't even sure of my client.

A warning bell sounded somewhere in the back of my brain. Eliciting trust was the art of the true manipulator, the art of a conman. But he hadn't tried to get anything out of me, had he? If I kept my armour on he never would. All I had to do was watch and wait.

Watch and wait.

I grabbed my car keys and sprinted down the stairs, banking on the fact that he would be strolling away, enjoying the balmy night air. It would be easy to spot someone in the deserted streets. I heard a car start up in nearby Darling Street. I got into the Daimler and followed the sound. Watching and waiting. As I edged round the corner I saw a Ford Laser pull up at the lights. It was the only car in the street. I grabbed the beanie from the glovebox and put it on, making sure to tuck all my distinctive red hair up into it. He had his blinker on, indicating a right turn. He'd be going up to Victoria Road. It was the only way out of Balmain by this route. There was more than one advantage to living on a peninsula. When the lights changed he turned right and I kept going straight through. I drove down to the roundabout and doubled back up Beattie Street.

By the time I got to Victoria Road there were three cars between him and me. That suited me fine.

He went left and so did I. Through Annandale, across Parramatta Road, heading for Newtown.

King Street, Newtown, was slow, even at this time of night. There were still people straggling about, coming out of the Toucan Tango and getting into nearby cars, happy to have danced half the night away. On darker street corners kids looked like they were about to do dangerous things with beer bottles.

The traffic dragged, finally coming out on the Princes Highway. We were heading south. I had enough gas to get to Wollongong and back but I hoped we wouldn't be going that far. It was 2 a.m. and it had already been a long night.

The traffic moved steadily, through St Peters and Tempe. We were heading for the airport. But no planes were taking off at this time of night. Or landing. Unless he'd made private arrangements.

But he didn't go into the airport, he pulled up at the Airport Hilton.

He entered the vestibule doors. Casual, light-stepped. If I'd been close enough I might have heard him whistling. When he disappeared from the foyer I entered. Walking in as if I owned the place, or at least rented a room there.

There was no-one in the lift foyer but one of the lifts was going up. I kept the other lift door open and waited till the first one stopped. Floor seven. Mrs Chen had said that seven was a lucky number. I got in the waiting lift and pressed the button.

When the lift arrived I waited to make sure the corridor was quiet. If I did happen to run into him it wouldn't matter. He seemed to find no explanation necessary when he turned up on my turf.

I walked along the corridor looking for a room that had light streaming out from under the door. And found it.

I stood to the side and put my ear to the door. There were two people in there talking Chinese. One of them was Ho.

The other was a woman.

I felt my cheeks flush. So what did I care that James Ho was in a hotel room in the middle of the night with a woman? Maybe she was his sister. Or his mother.

Sure, I thought, trying to find ways around the obvious.

The talking stopped and the light went out. I waited for a long while. No-one emerged from the room. Whoever was in there was in for the duration.

It was 4.30 a.m. I took the fire-escape and went back to the car. I didn't think anyone would be leaving that room much before 6.30.

Two hours sleep.

I dreamed of Thailand. I've never been there but I knew it exactly as if I had been there in another life. I could almost smell the garlic and coriander. There was a huge golden Buddha being carried along by millions of people. They had covered it in cheap plaster to hide the gold. Warlords were coming and the people were protecting their treasure. Like the monks who'd smashed shadow bones instead of the real thing.

I woke from that dream to a hot rosy dawn. It was 6.15 a.m.

Back up the fire-escape I went and waited. Not long this time.

At 6.33 precisely the door opened. And shut.

The woman flicked back her hair and walked towards the lifts. She was in her mid-twenties; expensive leather jacket and leather trousers. The air of a high-class prostitute. Very high-class. Her smile was noncommittal. I let her get in the lift first. She was used to that.

As she got into the cab waiting outside I heard her one word to the driver.

The word was Cabramatta.

I drove back along the long and dreary Princes Highway thinking about room service. In Sydney you could get just about anything to tickle your fancy. I wondered what James Ho's particular fancy was.

With the memory of the dream I went to the kids' toybox and got out their Texta colours. I coloured the key in red and green. Then put it in the box along with the Lego, water-pistols and bits of broken cars. It was in good company.

Then I rang the Airport Hilton and asked for James Ho. No one of that name was staying there. I tried Joel Cairo but that drew a blank as well.

For obvious reasons Valentine's Day never passed unnoticed by me. The messages in the paper made entertaining reading and this year I was particularly looking forward to reading them because, for the first time, I had placed one there. I hoped bank robbers read them as well. It was a long shot but better than no shot at all.

I went downstairs and bought the paper, and came back to bed to read it at my leisure. The front page detailed another Triad killing, this time in Cabramatta. It didn't say whether the victim had been wearing a tie or if two of his fingers were missing. But his head was. It had been chopped off.

I turned to the pages of Valentine messages and went straight to mine.

> Stunning New Year's Eve party, really went off with a bang. And such a financial success as well. I just love fiery affairs with daring men. Can I be your Valentine? I would love to hear all about your adventures. I'm a perfect listener and discretion is my middle name. Dragon Lady

It wasn't terrific but it was no worse than the other messages to bunnykins, little bears, and pussycats.

This was the first Valentine's Day for Steve and me but we wouldn't be spending it together. He was at a conference in Melbourne but he'd be back in time to go to yum cha on Sunday. He wasn't the type to put messages in the paper but I was hoping the day wouldn't go completely unnoticed by him.

There was a knock on the door. I put on my bathrobe and went to answer it.

It was Jack. Standing there with an armful of roses and a small package wrapped in gold paper. It didn't really suit him. He looked more at home lugging around crates of beer.

'Your birthday come early this year?' he asked, handing them to me.

'It's Valentine's Day. How come you missed all the fuss?'

'It's just 14th February as far as I'm concerned,' he said briskly. Jack wasn't really a hearts and flowers man. 'Have a good one anyhow.'

There were ten red roses, a metric dozen they were calling them in the shops. I put them in a vase and sat it on the lacquer table.

I unwrapped the little package. Inside were earrings. Diamond studs in an antique gold setting. I wasn't that keen on gold but the earrings were beautiful. There was a plain white card with a gold border. 'Diamonds are forever,' it said. 'Looking forward to Sunday.'

I was impressed. Steve had really surpassed himself.

'Why not?'

Lucy had been delighted to accept my invitation to meet James Ho but when I rang her on Sunday morning and told her it was yum cha at the Red Dragon she'd had a change of heart.

'Yum cha, chum cha' was the way she referred to it, and she wasn't coming because she was in bed with a hunky blond Swede and was planning on staying there all day.

She was more than willing to meet the guy with the cute bum but not today and not in Chinatown. His presence in the area had not gone unnoticed.

'What are they saying about him?' I asked, shifting the phone from one ear to the other.

They were saying that he was asking questions about certain people, including the Chen family. And he was taking a particular interest in Chinese antique dealers.

'What sort of questions?'

Lucy couldn't be any more specific than 'just nosing around'. They were calling him the Chinese detective.

I should have guessed Lucy wouldn't come down to Chinatown, even with the lure of a cute bum. She was bright, efficient, and full of fun. She was the best fighter in our karate class but she hadn't developed the clear mind and detachment of the Masters. Lucy fought with a hard concentration, as if wrestling with demons of her own. Though she operated with the world at large as an individual, as far as Chinatown was concerned she was simply a member of the Lau family, a piece that only had significance in relation to the whole. The only way she could remain an individual was to stay away from her background.

At moments like these I felt the strictures of family, but at other times I wondered if I didn't envy Lucy that solidarity. If my father had hung around longer I might at least have had a few brothers and sisters.

But. It did mean I could go to Chinatown for brunch without being bothered about the wagging tongues. And I'd fought so hard to have the life I had I doubted whether there was anybody in the world I'd allow to chip away at it.

I knocked on Steve's door.

'A belated Happy Valentine's Day,' I said, handing him a bottle of champagne.

'Mmm,' he said, kissing me, 'I'll save that for later.'

'The flowers were great and the earrings are just fantastic.'

'What earrings?' he asked, looking mystified.

'Oh come on, Steve, the ones I'm wearing.'

'Nice,' he commented. 'Where did you get them?'

'Wasn't it you?'

'No.'

'I must have a secret admirer then.'

'As long as he's only admiring,' said Steve. Then he smiled. 'If you find out who it is, see if you can get a pair for me as well.'

As we drove towards Chinatown I told Steve about Lucy.

'When you see her at work,' he said, 'you wouldn't even know she had a family. It's as if she'd sprung up autochthonously.'

'What?'

'Look it up in the dictionary.'

Sunday morning was relatively quiet and while I'd been prepared to park in one of the stations that had sprung up to keep pace with the Entertainment Centre, we found a space in the street near what used to be Paddy's Market. That site was presently inert, waiting to be made over into a hotel and conference centre. In my university days I used to come down here on Sundays, do the shopping for the household at Paddy's, and eat freshly made dim sims and lemon chicken at the Lean Sun Lo. Paddy's then was almost part of Chinatown, big and booming in the high-roofed hall, floor slippery with cabbage leaves and splashes of liquid best left uninvestigated. You could buy anything you wanted at Paddy's and a lot of what you didn't want.

Chinatown also had cabbage leaves and splashes of liquid but at least the garbage was organic. Now people walked along Dixon Street as if it were the Champs Elysées, to look and to be seen. The Lean Sun Lo was gone and the building had become an arcade of expensive clothes shops, an art gallery, and a flash Chinese herbalist. Upstairs where they used to gamble were offices. Though they probably still gambled up there.

But the Chinese still came on Sundays for yum cha.

James Ho was waiting at the small bar off the main eating area drinking something white. I introduced him to Steve. Like men who have a woman friend in common (though I still wasn't sure I could call Ho my friend) they were sizing each other up beneath the polite signals of introduction.

Ho asked us what we wanted to drink. I told him champagne and orange juice would be just fine.

Steve fingered his ear, a gesture I'd noticed on our first meeting in the pacemaker clinic several moons ago. I'd learned the significance of that gesture. It meant his brain was open for business and he wasn't going to let anything slip away unnoticed.

He wasn't the only one thinking about ears.

'Lovely earrings,' commented Ho. 'So glad you're wearing them.'

Diamonds are forever. Of course. It had to be James Ho.

There was an awkward lull in the conversation.

'You have only one friend?' Ho enquired, taking up the slack.

'One more than you have,' I retorted. 'They stayed away in droves when they knew you were coming.'

'You never know who might turn up later,' he said cryptically. 'What do you do in your life, Mr Angell?'

'Part of the time I'm a pacemaker technician. What about you?'

'I'm a detective. All of the time.'

'And what brings you to Sydney?'

'International enquiries.'

'Something that couldn't be taken care of locally?'

I gave Steve a sharp look but he was only making conversation.

'Chinese affairs are best taken care of by Chinese,' he said somewhat ironically. Steve excused himself, ostensibly to go to the toilet. He'd only had one drink.

'There are exceptions of course,' he added. 'But then the key wasn't found in Chinatown, was it?'

'You're telling the story. Where did you find it? I don't believe you got round to that.'

'In a gold shop.'

'How come I missed it?'

'Perhaps I was more thorough. I believe the Chinese gold diggers made quite a good living sifting through what the European diggers had already discarded. By the way, where is the key?'

'In a safe place. I've not yet handed it over to Mrs Chen, who, I'd like to remind you, is my client. Who are you working for?'

'Ah, here is Mr Angell back again.'

As Steve joined us a waiter came up. 'Miss Valentine?'

'Yes...' I said uncertainly.

'I took the liberty of booking in your name,' said Ho. 'I hope you don't mind.'

Mind? This was chicken-feed compared to some of the liberties he'd taken.

'Your client must like you,' said Ho smoothly. 'We have jumped the queue.'

'This is all?' asked the waiter as we approached a table large enough to seat ten. 'You are expecting other guests?'

I wasn't expecting anyone but I wasn't sure if James Ho was, not sure at all.

'No,' I said, 'this is it.'

'Perhaps later we can find you a smaller table. Many bookings today for yum cha.' He handed us the docket that would be marked up as we ate our way through dishes that girls brought round on trolleys.

The restaurant was full of family groups, and noisy. Ho had said it was as much a time for gossiping as it was for eating. The children were well-mannered and several little girls had red bows in their hair. The grandmothers tended to the children, presenting them with tidbits, while the mothers and fathers and aunts and uncles talked in high-pitched staccato tones.

One table was set up in a more grandiose style than the others and remained empty even though there were people lined up waiting to be seated.

A girl, who would have been no more than fifteen, trundled a trolley up to our table.

'Why don't you do the honours, James? I'll eat anything but chicken's feet.'

The list seemed to go on and on. Ho even ordered Chinese beer to go with it.

The girl returned and placed in the centre of the table steamed dumplings, barbecued pork, crispy noodles, wontons and vegetable spring rolls—for starters.

I had just taken the first bite from a pork bun when a party came from another entrance and sat down at the grandiose table. Among them were my clients, Charles and Victoria Chen. Though the table was round, Mrs Chen gave the impression she was sitting at the head of it. She was calm and gracious. There were no dockets on that table and they were served right away.

Equally graciously she bowed her head slightly in my direction, welcoming me to her restaurant. Her eyes caught slightly on Ho then the graciousness returned as she passed on to Steve.

I hadn't noticed where they'd come from, absorbed as I was in watching the Chen party, but suddenly we were joined by three youths. They could have been the brothers of the man-with-no-tie. Bangs of hair and long sideburns seemed to be the order of the day.

Ho picked up chopsticks though his bowl was empty.

A waiter came over looking flustered. He spoke to them in Chinese and judging by his tone of voice and gestures, pointing at the people waiting, and at us, it seemed he was asking them to leave. Steve now stopped eating and I centred myself in my chair, easing it out a little.

Ho sat there the same as before, seemingly disinterested but holding the chopsticks, and not as if he was about to eat with them.

One of the hoods picked up a pork bun and shoved it in the waiter's mouth. It didn't look good for the waiter to be eating on duty.

I wasn't very impressed—that was our pork bun he'd used.

The second hood picked up the noodles and threw them across the room where they landed unceremoniously a metre from Mrs Chen.

There was a sudden break in the conversation of the restaurant, a hyphen suspended in the air.

Mrs Chen stood up, her body taut. Her eyes glared like the eyes of a jaguar. She looked like she was about to breathe fire. A cook appeared, carrying a mean-looking meat cleaver. With one flick of her eyes Mrs Chen sent him back to the kitchen.

Into the silence sprang James Ho, the chopsticks now weapons that dug into the jugular vein of the guy who'd thrown the noodles. The pork bun thrower confronted Ho with a fist reinforced by a set of good old-fashioned knuckle-dusters. Ho swept the fist away and without even turning fully around kicked the third guy who had crept up from behind.

I was standing now, fists half-curled ready for action but it didn't look like my services were going to be required. Ho could handle an army of punks like these. Steve was also standing, more for moral support than anything else. He'd never hit anyone in his life. When you're that tall you don't have to. All you have to do is lean a little and the other guy falls over.

Mrs Chen didn't move from her table. The voice was enough. I didn't understand what it was she said to them but I didn't have to. The voice would have blown me clean out of the restaurant if it had been directed at me.

The one who'd thrown the noodles exposed the dragon tattoo on his forearm and said something in Chinese. Then they left.

The hum of conversation started up again like a disturbed hornet's nest, much more excited and feverish than before. If they'd come here for gossip they were certainly not disappointed. Ho sat down again and started on the wontons, which had remained untouched.

I noticed Mrs Chen was no longer at her table.

'Excuse me,' I said, more to Steve than to Ho.

As I passed through the kitchen on my way upstairs I noticed the cook with the cleaver wasn't there either.

I didn't like the look of him anyhow. He looked far too reptilian to be preparing food for human consumption.

The tight knife-pleats of Mrs Chen's blue dress came in and out like a concertina as she paced the room as far as the telephone cord would permit. I couldn't understand what she was saying but it sounded urgent. So urgent in fact that she'd neglected to close the door marked PRIVATE.

She hung up abruptly and went over to the window. Lonely as an emperor looking down on the peasants in the street.

She returned to the sideboard beneath the white-gauzed portrait and looked at it grimly. She said a few words to her departed husband. Probably along the lines of 'why did you leave me with all this mess?'

Bending down she slid her hand under the edge of the sideboard and withdrew a key. She unlocked the sideboard and took out a plain cardboard box, the sort you get in cake shops. She placed the box on the glass table and opened it up. Inside were fortune cookies. She closed the box and placed it on a sheet of red cellophane and made a pretty parcel of it. Then she put the parcel back in the sideboard.

She made another phone call, this time short, imperative. Like she was giving orders to a servant. As she hung up I stepped into view.

She became once again gracious. 'I'm sorry for the trouble at your table. Just naughty boys having some fun. Nothing to worry about. If you'll excuse me, I must get back to my table.'

I stood in the doorway, blocking her way.

'Excuse me,' she said, 'perhaps we can talk later.'

'Now will be fine for me, and it'll be just fine for you, too.'

'I do not have time now.'

'Then I'll give you five minutes of mine. You're paying for it. What was that all about downstairs?'

'I told you, just boys fighting. Nothing to worry about.'

I went to the phone and started dialling. 'I'm sure if it was nothing you won't mind me reporting it to the police. And stay away from the alarm button under the table; we don't want those cooks up here, do we?'

Her long fingers darted out and cancelled the call. 'No police,' she said urgently.

I put the phone down. 'Why not the police?'

'In Chinatown we look after out own affairs.'

She said it with conviction but I'd heard it once too often.

'I've had just about enough of this,' I exploded. 'Do you think you're living in purdah?' I cried, too annoyed to notice I was crossing cultures. 'The world extends beyond these streets, in case you hadn't noticed. That business downstairs was mine as much as yours. I was eating those pork buns and noodles. How well are you looking after your affairs if fights can break out in your own restaurant?'

Any other person would have been cowering under this onslaught. All Mrs Chen managed was to look bewildered. Probably the first time in her life anyone had spoken to her like this. Well, I hadn't finished yet. 'Who's paying those boys to mess up your waiters and chuck food all over the place? Who's pulling your strings, Mrs Chen?'

She stared back at me. Hesitated for a moment, on the edge. But she withdrew, regained her composure. I played my ace.

'I know where the key is,' I said.

Now it had become a different ball game. Her eyes lit up, eager. Then she cooled down again.

'When will you be able to deliver it?' she said, as if it was a piece of furniture.

'When you've answered a few of my questions.'

A man appeared at the door. She waved him away.

'It is imperative that you return the key.' She turned away

from me. 'It is a matter of life and death,' she said, almost in a whisper.

'Whose life and death?'

'I'm sorry, I cannot tell you more than this. Please return the key. You will receive a bonus. Then you can consider your engagement finished. You will not be further involved.'

'I'm not one of your servants, to dismiss at your whim. You want the key, you'd better come up with some answers. You know where to reach me.'

At the bottom of the stairs I waited. Everything in the restaurant was back to normal. I looked across at Steve and Ho. They were eating little custard tarts and drinking tea. They looked like they were doing fine without me.

The man who'd appeared at the door came down the stairs. He was carrying the red cellophane parcel.

I took out one of my cards, scribbled a note to Steve, grabbed a passing waiter and asked him to give it to him.

The man with the cellophane parcel left the restaurant by the back entrance. So did I.

In the narrow back alley was a car that looked oddly out of place amid the garbage bins. The white Mercedes with black tinted windows. The man beeped off the burglar alarm and got in.

I sprinted over to where my car was parked and waited. There was only one way out of that alley and he'd have to pass me.

He came by and I set the Daimler's engine purring. I watched him turn left out of Harbour Street into Pier, then followed.

There was traffic now between us. I was close enough to keep him in view, far enough away not to be obvious.

We drove past the Powerhouse Museum, and continued down the steep hill towards Wentworth Park, stopping at the lights at the bottom. I remembered how in the flash floods last spring this area had looked like Venice, the water right up to the buildings, covering both the road and footpaths. Cars ploughed through, sending up curved sheets of spray. Now it was a road again and the grass in Wentworth Park had turned brown.

The lights changed and the Merc continued. He was taking a well-worn path into Glebe, round Wentworth Park and into Bridge Road. Now side streets proliferated and the traffic thinned and fanned out as we came up to Glebe Point Road.

The Merc turned right. I was familiar with this stretch. Lots of Lebanese take-aways and one of the world's best book shops. Further up, on the other side of the road, was a motel. Beside the pool of this motel I'd once overheard a couple of well-oiled men in dark glasses and single earrings negotiating a drug deal. It was outside this motel that the Merc stopped.

I cruised past slowly. Through the rear-vision mirror I watched the chauffeur get out. With a shopping-bag. He looked about. Not furtively, but his eyes were taking in more than a casual glance. I parked the car and got out. There were a few people walking along but no-one took any notice of him. Except me.

He led me through a maze of back streets that got progressively leafier in keeping with the large houses down that end of Glebe. Then he came to a long brick wall topped by a terracotta Chinese tile trim. I darted into a particularly green garden and watched from the cover of a dark bush that had hard orange berries on it. A small bird fluttered up from it. The man looked about and walked to an entrance—a red ornamental gate, opened; a green lion either side sitting comfortably like domestic cats. The Sze Yap temple in Glebe. He went in.

I waited in the bush. It was a little cramped. I had dislodged a spider's web and the wispy bits were making my forehead itch. Thankfully it didn't take him long to go about his business. He was out again in under ten minutes.

Without the shopping-bag with the red cellophane parcel.

I waited till he had gone past then I entered through the gates.

The grounds formed a definite square, divided by the path leading in from the gates. One side was just lawn, or rather lawn and grass—only half of it had been mown and the mower sat where the lawn stopped and the grass started. On the other side of the path grew old peach trees and camellias. Behind them were banana palms and some big old eucalypts. There was a toilet block with signs, LADIES and GENTS. In English. The path led to what looked like a picnic area. There were chairs and tables and a sort of barbecue with an A-frame roof on it. There were blobs of candle wax on what would have been the barbecue plate and beside it a small furnace. Both were brick with red and green trimmings. They were places to offer prayers. Prayers going up to heaven in the smoke of incense or in paper burnt.

People were sitting at the tables chatting while some well-behaved kids in their Sunday best played near by. The chatting dropped away considerably when I came into view. I smiled at everyone, nice and easy, as if I was out on a Sunday stroll and had just happened to wander in.

It was a clear sunny day but without the heaviness of full summer heat. A good day for strolling.

In between the banana palms I spied the bright blue of a tarpaulin. Things hidden away in corners interested me. I walked closer.

The tarp was part of a makeshift abode. There were a couple of milk crates in the middle of the dirt floor, and a board on top of them on which was standing a pot with coffee caked in mud-coloured rivulets down the sides.

On a piece of foam rubber lay a sleeping figure. It wore jeans, its back was young and tender and streaming down the back was long curling brown hair. It was a hippie, a species long believed to be extinct. Perhaps, like Sleeping Beauty, it was waiting for one of its kind to give it the kiss of life. It wasn't going to be me. I would rather let sleeping hippies lie. There was no-one else about outside. Time to tackle the temple itself.

On the way I noticed a line strung with clothes too small to belong to Sleeping Beauty.

The temple was in three sections with a board that served as a walkway between them. I went into the section on the left. The walls were lined with photos of people, some script in Chinese but beside that were their names, and the years denoting their birth and death. I stopped at one photo and looked at it for a long time. The name told me it was John Chen and that he had died in 1987. A handsome man, in the photo he looked about twenty-five.

Someone else entered the temple. A man wearing an ordinary shirt and trousers. I don't know why that surprised me. Maybe I'd been expecting monk's clothes or something. He asked me if I wanted tea. I said yes. He walked out again without waiting.

He was sitting at a table beneath a big tree, away from the other visitors. I sat down with him, politely.

'Do you live here?' I asked.

'I am the manager. I work. Only the days.'

'Anyone else live here?'

'Sifu. The teacher. He lives upstairs.'

But there were children's clothes hanging on the line. Maybe they were going to the poor, to a St Vincent de Paul kind of shop. I thought of Lucy's father and his charity work. Of Mrs Chen and her committees.

'I saw a boy up the back.'

'A boy?'

'A young man. Near the banana palms. Asleep.'

'He works here. Gardener.'

I looked again at the lawn-mower stopped in mid-stream. He must have had a sudden urge to lie down.

'It's very peaceful here,' I remarked.

'It is the place of Buddha,' he said, slowly sipping his tea.

Buddha's temple. Perhaps I would find some interesting relics here.

I finished my tea, taking large but unobtrusive mouthfuls.

'Is it permitted to visit the rest of the temple?'

'It is like a church. Open to all sincere visitors.'

'Thank you for the tea.'

He bowed his head in acknowledgement. Maybe he should have been thanking me. He had served me tea. I had allowed him to accrue some brownie points in Buddha heaven.

I entered the central section. The smell of sandalwood pervaded the place. Everything was red and gold. Lanterns with tassels hung in crowded rows from the ceiling. It was nowhere near the size of a church, about the size of a largish bedroom. Up the front was an altar. I recognised the white statue of Kuan

Yin. There were other deities as well. Warlike deities. There were burnt-down incense sticks, flowers and sweets as offerings. I noticed some Minties.

There were a few chairs against the wall—marble seats in wooden frames. They looked like commodes. I tried one but the seat didn't lift.

It was not the place for a priest and congregation. You made your offering then went outside and had tea and gossip at the tables under the big tree.

By way of one of the boards I walked through to another section. It turned out to be some sort of office. A messy sort of office. Again, there was a coffee pot that looked as if it had stood in the same place for years. The whole place was taking on the allure of Sleeping Beauty's castle. I walked through to the third section of the temple.

This was smaller but the offerings were bigger. There were white hen's eggs and slices of fruit that had vinegar flies crawling over them. At the front was a painted cloth depicting the chief god of the temple in martial attire. On the right was the yang god, Kuan Ti, champion of kung fu and former idol of warlords and emperors. On the left was Kuan Yin, sometimes known as the queen of heaven. She had offerings in front of her.

In particular she had a red cellophane parcel.

I looked at her face and her out-turned palms offering me infinite mercy and compassion. I hoped there was forgiveness in them too for what I was about to do.

I picked up the parcel. I felt like I was robbing the collection box.

I had time only to loosen one end of the shiny red ribbon before I saw him. Coming from behind the screen.

A monk in maroon robes.

His face was placid but his body was ready for action.

I ran. With the parcel. Out of the temple and into the yard. Suddenly the castle had come to life. An image flashed past like a scene observed from a fast-moving train. A child's face in an upstairs window of the temple, a child about the same age as

Amy. It only lasted a second. The child's mouth started to open in surprise then she was gone and a curtain had been drawn. The clothes on the line. I was running hard. Towards the wall. My pursuer was closing in. My veins filled with adrenalin. I felt as if I could fly.

I was making my run-up to the wall when I felt a hand grab my heel. I was coming down to the ground. Slowly. I had time to see the world flash by, as if I were falling from a great height. Before I hit the ground I flung the parcel over the wall. I struck out wildly with my now freed hands but I was only hitting air. There was no-one there. Whoever had grabbed my foot wanted the parcel, not me. What was in it that the whole temple had gone on red alert the minute I'd touched it?

Was Mrs Chen hiding something in there? Transferring it to the protective custody of the temple?

I ran back out the open gates. The parcel had split and fortune cookies were strewn across the street. But there were rapidly fewer and fewer of them. They were being picked up by the man in maroon. I tried to join in but was pushed aside. He was like a dog protecting a bone. I felt the skin of my knee grazing against the hard bitumen. My hands grazed as well as I landed flat on the road. Beneath one hand I felt some lumps. Cookies. I curled my hand aroung them and before the maroon-shrouded leg could make contact I lurched up and ran.

Once back in the safety of numbers in Glebe Point Road I took out the fortune cookies I'd managed to retrieve. Similar to the one I'd been handed at the Lantern Festival. I broke the first one open. There was no message in it. I broke open the second. Nothing. I dropped the cookies into a garbage bin.

As I approached my car I noticed someone slouching against it. He was wearing sunglasses and had his hands in the pockets of his jean jacket. I couldn't be sure but he looked like one of the guys who'd caused trouble in the restaurant. When he spotted me he stood up straight and walked briskly down a side street.

I sprinted up to the car. There were no broken windows or any visible damage. I followed down the street in time to see him disappear in the direction of the temple. I went all the way back there looking for him but he was nowhere to be seen.

I walked back up to Glebe Point Road, feeling my grazed knees with every step.

The white Merc was gone.

I went back to the Daimler and drove off.

Steve was watering his courtyard jungle when I got back to Newtown.

'How did you go?'

'Robbed a church. Lightning struck. How about you?'

'Your secret admirer was very entertaining. And informative. Said he'd been up to your room.'

Water dripped off the ferns. The earth soaked it up audibly. Little hissing sounds as it drank.

'Not invited though.'

'I'm surprised you're still talking to him.'

He'd turned the tap off now and was pulling at odd weeds that came easily out of the damp soil.

'The way you go on about your "space", as if your room is hallowed ground. I thought no-one got into your room without an invitation.'

'You need some snail pellets.'

'The soil in Newtown is poisonous enough. I'd rather come out here at night and trample them to death. It wasn't just the once, was it?'

'What?' I'd been pulling out the odd weed myself but now I stood up.

It was Steve's garden.

'Him coming to your room.'

'C'mon, Steve, he's just a pesky little mosquito.'

'That's not the impression I got,' said Steve darkly, 'seems to be a pretty smart operator. And not at all bad looking, if you like that type. What's he doing here anyhow?'

'You tell me. Since he was so "informative".'

'I didn't know you were working on a case together. In fact you never mentioned him before the yum cha invitation.'

'You don't tell me all the details of your job. And besides, I'm not working with him, he just seems to turn up all the time.'

'Bearing gifts.'

I could feel the earrings burning holes in my ears.

Steve said nothing.

I sighed. 'Look, this is stupid. I don't invite him, he just turns up. Do you think I should get a restraining order put on him?' I quipped.

Steve didn't laugh. Instead he made loops of the hose and neatly placed it back around the tap.

'Want to go to the pub?' he said suddenly. 'I feel like getting sloshed.'

'On a Sunday night?'

'The hospital can pay for the hangover.'

He walked past me into the bathroom and washed his hands. He put on a T-shirt and slapped his arm. 'Mosquitoes are particularly bad this summer, aren't they?'

I smiled. The little black cloud had lifted. 'Will we go to Jack's?'

I was careful not to say *my* pub.

George was there in full swing, rocking from his toes to his heels. He didn't even know he was doing it. But he never spilt a precious drop of alcohol.

'G'day, Steve,' said Jack with a nod of his head, 'what'll you have, mate?'

'Double Scotch.'

Jack poured a double, and single for me. We took them away to the table in the corner. The white noise of the pub was a good background against which to think. The image of the girl's face at the window kept coming back. I held it in my mind and tried to scan every inch of it. It was out of place. I shouldn't have seen it. Why else would the curtain have come across so suddenly?

In Nepal they have a Living Goddess who lives from the age of six till puberty in the temple in Kathmandu. It is a great honour, especially for the parents of the chosen child, but at puberty she becomes 'impure' and must leave. She usually ends up as a prostitute. No-one wants to marry an ex-Living Goddess.

But the face at the window wasn't a Living Goddess, it was just a little girl.

And what of the guy leaning against my car? He'd walked away as soon as he'd seen me. How did he know it was my car? Had I been so intent on following the man in the white Merc that I'd missed someone following me?

There were a lot of questions going through my mind but no answers. But I knew who might have them. Mrs Chen.

Steve came back to the table with his second Scotch. Mine was hardly touched.

'Well you're a packet of laughs,' he said.

'Pardon?'

'Precisely. I thought at least you'd keep pace with me.'

'Sloshed yet?'

'Not enough.'

'While you can still remember things I'd like to make you an offer. How would you like to earn a bit extra on the side? Get back on the game?'

'I'm not going to stand on a street corner in a miniskirt for anyone.'

'Not that game. Your old one. The one you were doing in Germany. There'd be a quid in it. Make a change from listening to hearts.'

'Who do you want me to bug?'

'Mrs Chen,' I said, finishing off my Scotch. 'Ready for another?'

'I will be by the time you come back with them.'

I walked towards the bar. George raised his glass to me. The bar was two rows deep now. There are times when being tall and knowing the barman has advantages. This was one of them. I held up a five dollar note, letting Jack know we wanted another round.

'I'm going cheap,' said a guy sitting on a nearby barstool.

'Mind you don't fall off your perch,' I retorted.

'Sorry I spoke,' he said in mock apology.

When the drinks came he was the one to hand them to me. And it gave him great patronising pleasure.

I breezed past him, back to Steve.

'Why?'

'Because you said you wanted to get pissed.'

'Why Mrs Chen? You want me to bug your client?'

'Because I'm not getting any information out of her through the regular channels. She's like Fort Knox. I've asked her polite questions, I've asked not so polite questions. What we saw at yum cha is just the tip of an iceberg. It's the other eight-ninths I want to know about. She makes phone calls. There's something going on that she's not telling me about, just dismisses me like a servant.'

'Now that would get Claudia Valentine's dander up, wouldn't it?' said Steve amused.

I grunted. 'OK,' I admitted, halfway between a smile and a grimace, 'so she is employing me, but if she thinks she can treat me like a hired hand she's got another think coming. I've got what she thinks is her key and I'm going to keep it till she can convince me she's the person who should have it.'

Steve was looking at me with those beautiful eyes that had hooked me in the first place. He could barely suppress a grin and didn't look like he was even trying.

I gave up. We sat for a moment examining the bottoms of our glasses.

'Well? Are you going to do it?'

'Try sweet-talking me.'

'You think I'm going to sit here with my front paws up...'

'I'd rather the back paws.'

George lurched by and gave me one of his lecherous winks. That was all I needed.

'They've killed another one of them,' he said gleefully.

'Yes, George,' I sighed. I could smell his breath. Something about it reminded me of paint stripper.

'Another little yellow bastard.' He often went on about the little yellow bastards. George had never really come back from the war. 'Cabramatta. Hacked to pieces with a meat cleaver.'

I started to pay attention. 'Where did you hear about this, George?'

'On the television. Hacked to pieces,' he repeated, as he moved on to tell the next person who caught his eye.

I went over to the bar and called Jack aside.

'You watch the news this evening?'

'They'd mutiny if I didn't put it on.'

'What happened at Cabramatta?'

'Another one of those Triad killings apparently. Particularly nasty piece of work this time. Chopped up like satay chicken. Must have been a fight. They found the hand. It still had the knuckle-dusters on it.'

Knuckle-dusters. One of the hoods at yum cha had been wearing knuckle-dusters.

I went back to Steve. 'How soon can you start?'

'I've made up my mind, have I? OK, OK,' he said, when he saw I had made up mine, 'I'll do it, I'll do it. It'll cost you a bit. Those Telecom boys don't come cheap. And there's the equipment, tapes and stuff.'

'Mrs Chen's money will be paying for it. Expenses. Sort of ironic really, paying to have your own phone bugged. It'll hardly be a drop in her ocean of money.'

'You want another?'

I sighed heavily. 'No thanks, I need the one remaining brain cell. I've got some serious thinking to do. If you want to keep going why don't we get a bottle and take it up to my room?'

'Why didn't I ever meet women like you in my youth?'

'Because women like me weren't born then.'

Steve stood up. 'I'll get a half. I've changed my mind about getting sloshed. This is going to be a night to remember.'

It certainly was a night to remember.

Steve's words echoed hollowly the minute I opened the door. I knew even before I turned the light on. I motioned to Steve to stand back. I knew what had happened but I had to turn the light on to assess the extent of it.

It was a mess. Even my kids in an unchecked three day binge couldn't have made a mess like this.

The french doors were open like a gaping wound.

Then I took in the rest. My lacquer boxes were all over the floor, the books out of the bookcase, the toys all over the place.

The key, of course, was gone.

As far as I was aware only three people knew I had that key. Steve, James Ho and Mrs Chen. I hissed the last name out through my teeth.

The phone was still intact. I rang the restaurant. Mrs Chen had left.

'How soon can you start the phone tap?'

'Tomorrow. You want just the restaurant or the home as well?'

'Both. Think the home's in St Ives. Unlisted number. I'll let you know when I've got it.'

'Want me to give you a hand with this?'

'No,' I said grimly, 'not yet. I might be able to get some mileage out of it. Maybe bring Carol in. Break and enter. See how Mrs Chen likes that.'

I also wanted to piece the break-in together. See whose style it was. Maybe it wasn't organised by Mrs Chen at all. I was too angry to think straight at the moment. Maybe in the morning I would find a print of an expensive Italian leather shoe. I narrowed my eyes, looking at the french doors. This was not Ho's style. Whoever had done this wasn't fussy about cleaning up afterwards. Ho would have done it without a trace. And why would he steal back the key he'd given me in the first place? Was this what he meant by 'moving things along'? If it was, I wasn't the least bit impressed.

I went out on the balcony and looked back in at the mess. Steve was standing in the middle of it, perfectly still.

'Would you like to sit down?'

'Where?'

'Well there's not a lot of choice. On the bed. Make yourself at home.'

He shrugged. 'I might just tiptoe into the kitchen first. You got a couple of drinking vessels?'

The kitchen! I hadn't even thought to look there. We went in together. It was just as I'd left it. The bathroom was the same. Not even a white nurse's shoe peeping round the corner of the shower recess. It was only this room, the space where I live, that had been invaded.

Steve offered me an inch of Scotch. 'In a minute,' I said.

He sat on the bed which was unmade but in a different way from how I'd left it that morning.

The pot plants on the balcony were all in order. Why hadn't I buried the key in one of them? But maybe they would have gone through the pot plants too if they hadn't come across the key where they did.

In through the door. The lacquer boxes first. Across the table. Then the drawers opened, papers and clothes strewn about. Books off the shelves. Cassettes out of their covers. Vince Jones was still there and so was my unmarked tape of the Chen interview. Then the kids' toybox. They'd rifled my children's toybox.

That violation. My children's things strewn all over the place. Innocent little bits of Lego and the water-pistols. And my stuff. All over the place. My private space.

'Claudia,' said Steve softly.

'Look, I . . .' I raised my hands helplessly. My voice was quivering and I could feel my breath getting short.

As I walked back in I bumped my grazed knee on the table. My armour was wearing very thin. Just about threadbare. I slumped down on the floor and held my hand up to my face.

'Hey, Magnum . . .' Steve's soothing voice. His arms around me, holding me against him.

'Do you want me to ring Carol?' he said softly.

I shook my head against his chest. I was past anger now. The day had been full of unpleasant events and I'd had enough. I just wanted to crawl into that unmade bed and be enfolded in angel's wings.

I sniffed and wiped my hand across my face.

'Say, is that a gun you're sitting on or are you just pleased to see me?' Steve felt under my leg and produced Amy's water-pistol.

For some reason I found it hilarious and broke into fits of laughter.

'I think I'll have that drink now,' I said, going for the glasses Steve had poured.

We drank them down in one go. It felt like a warm bath.

I started taking off my clothes. So did Steve.

I was down to bra and pants. They both would have slipped off easily but I had other plans.

I leant over Steve who was now on the bed and said, 'Having a bit of trouble with this, do you think you can be Southern gentleman and help a lady out of her trouble?'

Or at least her bra.

He brought his hands up around my back and with an expert movement released my breasts from their confinement. They were so close to his face I could feel his warm breath on them. He dipped a finger in the Scotch and drew slow circles around my nipples. The Scotch felt cold on them but that wasn't the reason they were standing to attention. They weren't cold for long. His mouth was on one, and the tips of his fingers, touching, barely touching, the other. His tongue played over one then the other. I rubbed my stomach against his nether regions, so soft on the outside, so hard within. All I could wish for was that he have two mouths. But I was in no hurry.

'Can I give you a refill?' I asked.

'As often as you like,' he murmured.

We clinked our glasses. 'It's a pleasure having you here.'

'You haven't had me yet, and the pleasure's just beginning,' Steve said huskily.

'Got something in your throat?' I enquired.

'Not yet.'

I moved onto my side, facing him now full frontal. Propping my elbow on the pillow.

Something went crunch. Ever so slightly. I stopped looking at Steve and looked under the pillow.

'Tsk, tsk, Claudia, crumbs in the bed.'

It was, or it had been, a fortune cookie. Now it was a flat little circle of crumbs. With a message. *If you chase the dragon beware the sting of its tail.*

The same message I'd been given at the Lantern Festival.

I went over to my wardrobe and felt in the pocket of the jacket I'd been wearing that night. There was nothing in it, except the ticket for the monorail. The message was now under my pillow.

I needed to sleep on it. Let my ever vigilant subconscious take it all in and make a pattern out of it. My conscious brain had had about enough.

I gathered up the bits of fortune cookie, drawing them together with the palm of my hand. Steve watched the operation intently.

'You leave all that mess on the floor and you clean up these crumbs? What about the evidence for Carol?'

'You know how I feel about crumbs in the bed. I'll put them back almost exactly as they were. And tell her it was my elbow that did the smashing. Meanwhile I'm going to sleep on it.'

'You very nearly did,' said Steve.

I ran a soft slow finger down from the hollow of his neck, all the way down to the navel, circling the nipples. He put his hands behind his head and lay back. I hoped he wasn't thinking of England. I would sleep on it. Meanwhile there was some pressing business to hand.

I **sat up** in bed with my cup of heart-starter and watched Steve dress for work. He wasn't fussy about what he wore. No-one ever looked under the white hospital coat. Or so he told me. In any case he was early enough to call back home to Newtown if he wanted to change. As he stooped down to put on his shoes he knocked one of the lacquer boxes. He put it back exactly as it had been. It didn't matter. I wasn't going to call the cops. But I might make Mrs Chen think I had. I leaned over to the phone and rang the Red Dragon. Mrs Chen was not in.

Steve bent down to kiss me and I smelled his warm-bread smell.

'See you later, Magnum.'

'Goodbye, Mr Angell, look me up any time you're in town.'

The door clicked and Steve was gone. I stretched out in the still-warm bed.

I liked this moment, the room back to myself again but the fresh memory of Steve in it. The warm bed, warm as toast. That made me think of crumbs. I was glad I didn't have to go to work in the ordinary sense of the term but I had to go to work anyway. First thing I had to do was clean up this mess.

I put the boxes back together, the books in the shelves, the toys in the box, the cassettes in their covers. All present and accounted for. Except for the key. If it was Mrs Chen, I could imagine she'd be none too pleased when she found out it was the false key. All that for nothing.

I rang the restaurant again. Mrs Chen would not be in today. She was sick.

I rang my Telecom contact.

'Drusilla? Claudia. Victoria Chen. Unlisted number. St Ives. Number and address.' I waited while she keyed it in. Whenever I rang Drusilla at work I knew better than to make small talk with her. Telecom was 'cost-effective'. The less time their operators were on air the better. The operators were bugged occasionally as well, although Telecom called it 'monitoring'.

'Nothing? Try J. Chen, John.'

That did the trick. I wrote the number and address down. 'I'll call you out of hours and we can have a decent chat, OK?'

As soon as I put the phone down it rang. It was Collier, telling me I had a stack of Valentine messages waiting for me. 'Thanks Brian, I'll come in and collect them straight away... I see. What time will you be back? OK, see you about two.' I wasn't in any hurry to collect them on Mrs Chen's behalf. But I was curious. Like anybody, I wanted to meet the brains behind the operation. Not that I was holding out much hope. It would probably turn out to be just like the pub. No genuine offers.

I rang Steve at work. He had set up the bugging of the Red Dragon. I gave him the Chens' home number. He told me again about the cost.

'A week ought to do it,' I said, 'maybe just a couple of days.'

I rang the St Ives number. A servant answered. Mrs Chen was sick. 'Sick or not available?' Sick, the servant repeated.

St Ives is a large leafy suburb with large leafy properties. The Chen residence covered two hectares. I pressed the buzzer at the security gates and said I had an Interflora delivery. I expected they were going to direct me to a tradesman's entrance but the gates clicked and opened.

It was about eleven o'clock in the morning and the sun was shining. It had been shining for days. It felt more like a steady hammering. I was wearing my blue suit with a dark blue shirt. I had black high heels to slip on when I got out of the car. I was clean, neat and sober, and I didn't care who knew it. I was everything the well-dressed Interflora delivery girl should be. I was calling on a sick lady.

The Daimler almost seemed to drive itself up the driveway. Some time in a former life it would have lived in a place like this. I hoped I wasn't going to have any trouble getting it back out again. There was a fleet of expensive cars to keep it company, including the white Merc.

I pulled into a white gravel parking area and slipped on the black shoes. I got out of the car carrying the red roses. The gift of love.

I wasn't particularly thinking of love as I crunched up to the entrance doors of the Chen residence. I was thinking more of the thorns.

Till I looked up. In the stained glass above the doors was Kuan Yin. It seemed like only yesterday since I'd last seen her—and it was.

I gazed at her for a long time till it seemed she was gazing back at me. That powerful calm.

There was no-one about, the place was as quiet as a cemetery and about the same size. But I felt the eyes of the house on me.

I brought my attention back to the door and pressed a buzzer.

They must have been standing behind it waiting, it opened so quickly.

'Interflora for Mrs Chen,' I said.

'Thank you,' replied a Chinese girl dressed up like a French maid. She moved her hand towards the roses. I moved them imperceptibly out of reach. 'There's a message. To be delivered personally.'

'Wait one moment,' she said, and started to close the door.

I stepped in sideways and the door now completed its closure behind me. 'I'll wait inside,' I said evenly.

The girl was about to protest but the open mouth quickly turned to a smile of acquiescence.

'One moment, please.'

You could have held a state reception in the vestibule—if there hadn't been so much furniture about, mostly decorative, not functional. It was all expensive though, and ornate. It was a bit like the chinoiserie section of the Victoria and Albert Museum. It was a pity John Chen had died before he'd gone into the antiques business. He'd gathered enough stock for it.

It was not Victoria but Charles Chen who came to receive me. He wasn't looking all that well himself. I hoped whatever was going on around here wasn't contagious. His clothes weren't too bad, it was the rest. He looked somehow drained, as if he'd been out all night. His hair wasn't gelled, and stuck up like porcupine spines. The boy looked worried.

And confused.

'I thought...'

'You thought I was an Interflora delivery person. But I do have flowers. For your mother.'

'Thank you,' he said, offering to relieve me of my load.

I repeated the gesture I'd made at the door with the French maid. No-one but Mrs Chen was going to prick their hands on these flowers.

'I'm afraid my mother is...you see there's been...'

'Thank you, Charles.'

She was dressed like a character out of *Dynasty*, completely in black, including the sunglasses. The sun was shining outside but it was by no means bright in here. Maybe she was going to a funeral. But black wasn't the Chinese colour for mourning.

'Miss Valentine?' she said, implying with her voice that I was to follow her.

I followed, still with flowers in hand, into a relatively small room with heavy red curtains. Just the two of us.

'Please excuse the glasses, I have a headache.'

Images of my violated room flashed before my eyes.

'Heard you were sick. But that's not why I'm here. It's about my room.'

'Yes,' she said, perfect even in her indisposition, 'I'm terribly sorry for any inconvenience caused.'

Inconvenience! I couldn't believe it. She'd had my room ransacked and she was apologising for the inconvenience.

'I'm sorry for the inconvenience too, the inconvenience you're going to have when the police call on you.'

'In what way are the police going to inconvenience me? Thank you,' she said to the maid who brought in coffee with the same little dragon cups that had been with us on our first interview. They didn't look so cute now. Or exquisite. The conversation stopped till the girl left the room. At least she recognised her servants had ears.

'Milk?'

'They will be round asking questions,' I said, not touching my coffee. 'They might also want to know about your cook.'

'My cook?'

'The one with the meat cleaver.'

'Ah.'

She was too calm. Floating.

'Take off the glasses, Mrs Chen.' I said softly.

She obliged like an obedient child. The eyes were bloodshot as hell and not focused. It looked to me like more than Valium.

'Would you like the police to ask you questions about the cook?'

'The key,' she said, and sighed briefly. 'You must find the key. Be a good girl and find the key.'

'No, Mrs Chen, I will not find the key. I have taken myself off the case. I am no longer your hired hand. Find someone else to run round in circles.'

I was in the vestibule trying to get out. It was locked from the inside. I'd made a stunning exit but was still stuck in the house.

Charles to the rescue. Or so I thought.

'My mother is. . .sick, she has taken. . .medication. . .' The Chen cool didn't extend to the son. If he'd been a nail-biter they would have been down to the quick by now. He had more nervous energy than he could contain. 'You must find the key, it is imperative.'

'That's what your mother said, but I'm afraid imperatives have lost their charm. Would you kindly let me out of this house?' I looked at the ornate furniture. It didn't buy you peace of mind.

Mrs Chen floated into the vestibule. 'Charles, let Miss Valentine out. She has to find the key.'

Charles looked like he was about to go down on his knees and beg me.

'Open the door, Charles.'

'Tell her, for Christ's sake, tell her!'

Open the door, Charles.'

Helplessly he opened the door, his assertiveness limited to one outburst.

I was out. Onto emerald-green pastures that looked like they'd been manicured rather than mown.

I got back in the Daimler, took off my high heels and drove away.

Instead of heading west when I got to the city side of the Bridge I went east. To the Botanic Gardens. A breath of relatively fresh air.

I swung the car down past St Mary's Cathedral. A wedding party was there, the bride and groom and the rest of them getting their photos taken on the steps. There were lots of hats about and everyone exuded an air of money. I hoped they would live happily ever after.

I parked the car and entered the Gardens. The joggers were fitter now than they used to be and shorts were shorter. I liked that.

Office girls and boys were sitting on the grass eating their sandwiches and getting a weekday tan. I strolled past a pond that had an island of wilderness in the middle of it. Ducks swam by silently, gliding along the surface while their webbed feet paddled through the murky brown water. I headed down to the blue water, the harbour with its rock wall. A young woman came along the walkway pushing a pram. Just like an English children's storybook with nannies in the park. Except in English storybooks you don't have harbours like this. There was traffic out there, speedboats and the odd windsurfer. From this angle the Bridge was huge and arched like an old-fashioned amusement arcade. The water was the colour of my shirt and there wasn't too much garbage in it. It was all fairly picturesque, the only eyesore the green and red floating restaurant that reminded me of something David would make with his Lego when he was feeling particularly perverse.

It was a long way from Chinatown and even further from St Ives.

I'd walked out of the Chen house and off the Chen case. I didn't care about their troubles any more or what it was Mrs Chen had to, for Christ's sake, tell me. Such a lot of trouble for one little key. It might well have been lying at the bottom of this very patch of water I was looking at. That was one theory, that the robbers had dumped the load in the harbour.

An hour later I was still thinking about it all. Out of the Chen house but maybe not off the case. It was like leaving off reading a good book because you didn't like one of the characters. I was curious, curious to know how it turned out. The only way to do that was to keep reading.

There'd been a few more additions since the last time I'd visited the State Library. On Macquarie Street, alongside the old yellow-brown sandstone building was a new glass and marble one. You could see white painted metal staircases inside. I thought I'd approach the old from the new and went up to the automatic circular doors. I had to wait a full half minute before the inner part would open, a subtle hint perhaps not to try and do a runner here with any books.

Inside was like a hotel reception area. Mushroom pink carpets and dark blue vinyl lounge chairs, and a circular information desk.

I melted into the chairs for minute to take it all in. Then I walked up the stairs, round and about, and down more stairs to come out to the entrance of the old Library.

In books lie the soul
of the whole past time
the articulate audible
voice of the past
when the body
and material substance
of it has altogether
vanished like a dream

I saw Tasman's inlaid map and walked on the strip of grey carpet over the surrounding ocean. There were even cherubim breathing out wind to give the ships fair sail.

The old section of the Library had received a new lease of life as well. There was now carpet inside and smart dark red filing cabinets. At the entrance were two tasteful displays of pink, grey, and black silk flowers in large vases, no doubt fashioned by one of our leading craftspeople. On commission. There was a lot of money going around for such things in 1988.

Books still lined the walls, their various colours like tiny pieces in a huge stained-glass mural. Above them light filtered down from pale pink and blue glass ceiling panels.

Getting into the computer catalogue was a bit like trying to get information out of Mrs Chen. You knew there must be something there but it kept going blank when you asked the wrong question.

Nothing came up for 'key'. Nothing came up for 'Triad'. Something came up for 'Chen' but it was 'Ch'en' and all historical. All that came up for 'puzzles' were kids' ones. 'Dragon' brought up *Chinese ornament: the lotus and the dragon*, and *The Dragon: nature of spirit, spirit of nature*. 'Tong' and 'secret societies' brought up the following—*Primitive revolutionaries of China: a study of secret societies in the late nineteenth century*; *The sociology of secret societies*; and *Tong in Cheek* (Cherry Delight Thrillers).

At the desk I went through the rigmarole of filling out the order slips and waiting. A twenty minute delay. There was a hush like I couldn't believe, the light grey carpet absorbing any stray sighs and grunts. The other readers were a mixed bunch, people who were in there because they liked books, others because they liked information.

Twenty minutes. There were better ways of filling in time than watching other people read. The computer wasn't the only way to get information. Its store of knowledge was greater than mine and it had a fantastic memory. But it didn't have legs and it didn't know it was in a library surrounded by books. I did and I was.

I walked to the shelves and took out some dictionaries of symbols. I was looking for keys, and boxes, preferably Buddha boxes.

There was nothing under 'boxes' but the other entry made interesting reading. And it wasn't all irrelevant.

'The key was a power to open the heavens and hells of many early religions and an attribute of numerous early deities.' It figured largely in all cultures and in all mythologies, including Christian. 'Power of keys' referred to Matthew xvi, 19 and the ecclesiastical authority of popes. It rested on a key. Jesus said to Peter, 'I will give unto thee the keys of the kingdom of heaven.' Is that why the Chen family remained influential? The power of the key?

I looked for instances of keys in Chinese folklore.

'A key is always given to an only son to lock him into life.'

Charles Chen was an only son. And he was a nervous boy. Was it his life and death that the key affected? Did he have some curious disease that could only be comforted by that dragon key? Could the gold of that key help his 'illness' in the same way that copper bracelets were supposed to ease arthritis?

Another dictionary told me that locks had been in existence since 2000 BC. More significantly, 'in the sixteenth century the combination lock, borrowed from the Chinese, came into vogue for jewellery boxes and safes'. Boxes for keeping treasures hidden, holy relics even.

But a combination lock didn't require a key.

So why did James Ho want a description of the Chens' key? A *detailed description of the key*.

I went to the serials section and sifted through *China Reconstructs* till I came to the November 1987 issue. All the same information was there as in the photocopy that Ho had given me. But there was more.

There were photos of the Buddha boxes. They were indeed opulent and fitted the descriptions given in the written word. I looked at the photos closely. It was a great pity they didn't show all sides of the boxes.

Because there was one detail missing.

My pile of books came from the stacks. A small pile. There were only three books—the revolutionaries, the sociology, and Cherry Delight. I would save Cherry for dessert.

The sociology told me that the Triad Society began when monks at a monastery named Shao-lin chih helped the Manchu government defeat a small but formidable kingdom. All one hundred and eight monks were subsequently persecuted by jealous government officers, but five of them resolved to form a secret society in order to dethrone the Manchus. They were a fighting order and practised what became kung fu.

They started off as Robin Hood type bandits; all men were brothers in the Triad, regardless of rank in the outside world. The book quoted one of the Triad 'poems':

> After joining the Hung Men (the Triad), I find that all members are brothers,
> I am not covetous of money nor greedy of other's offers,
> So kind that you, my brother, come to initiate me,
> How could I forget your mercy and betray the Family.

Primitive Revolutionaries told the same story and more. There was a long glossary of terms in the back, among them euphemisms for killing—'wash the body', and 'wash the face' which translated into 'cut off the head'. A hand was described as a five-clawed dragon.

It also gave the procedural details of a Triad initiation ceremony, which often took place in a temple. I found that interesting. For the initiation ceremony the temple was called the City of Willows and represented the flight of the five from the Manchus.

The recruits had to go through stages to get to the altar where the ceremony was completed.

As I looked at the plan of the City of Willows I thought of the temple in Glebe. The altar in Glebe was on the southern side of the temple but that didn't mean it couldn't be moved to suit the occasion.

The temple could easily be transformed into a Triad City of Willows.

For that matter, so could any room with four walls.

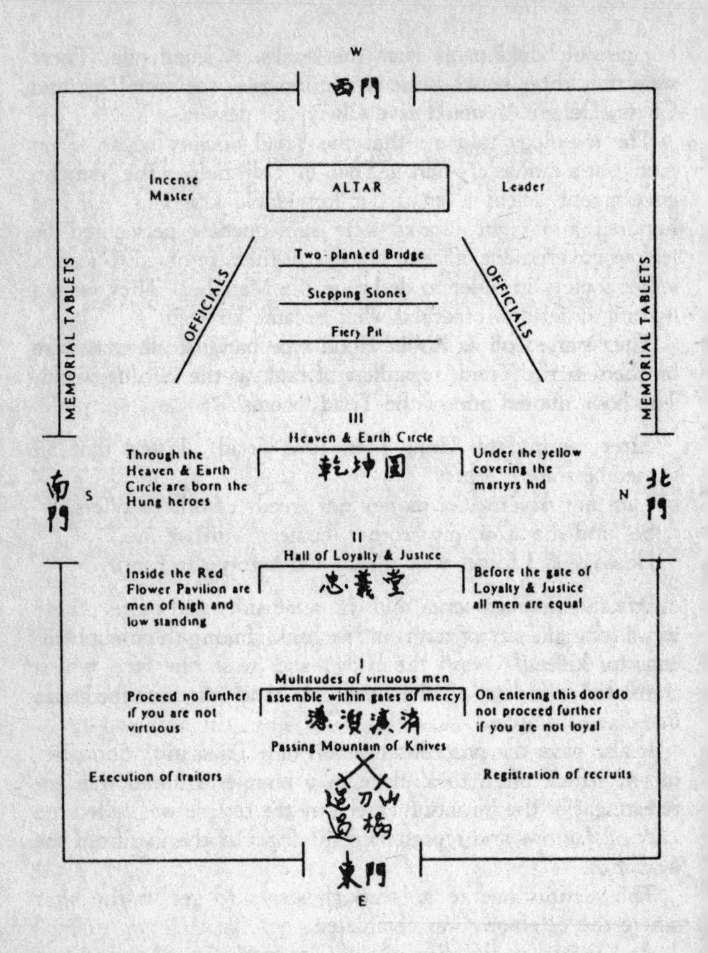
W
西門
Incense Master
ALTAR
Leader
OFFICIALS
Two-planked Bridge
Stepping Stones
Fiery Pit
OFFICIALS
MEMORIAL TABLETS
MEMORIAL TABLETS
III
Heaven & Earth Circle
乾坤圈
Through the Heaven & Earth Circle are born the Hung heroes
Under the yellow covering the martyrs hid
南門
S
N
北門
II
Hall of Loyalty & Justice
忠義堂
Inside the Red Flower Pavilion are men of high and low standing
Before the gate of Loyalty & Justice all men are equal
I
Multitudes of virtuous men assemble within gates of mercy
Proceed no further if you are not virtuous
On entering this door do not proceed further if you are not loyal
Passing Mountain of Knives
Execution of traitors
Registration of recruits
東門
E

I came to the last offering, *Tong in Cheek*. There was a photo on the cover of a woman in a wig and false eyelashes, baring a breast and a revolver. The blurb said:

> I'm Cherry Delight and I'm good at what I do. No boast, just fact. With revolver or automatic I can put six out of six in a bullseye, or a body. My hair is naturally red—hence the Cherry—and a Delight is what I am for people I like, or those I want to destroy. . . I love sex and I hate the Mob. . . I can speak six languages and kill without saying a word.

Cherry turned out to be a sharpshooting, rooting tooting bimbo; mainly rooting. As far as she was concerned the Tongs were just another version of the Mob, just as shootable, just as rootable.

The Library was no place for Cherry's delights.

When I walked back over the ocean of Tasman's map Detective Sergeant Jim Campbell was waiting. In plainclothes—a light grey windcheater, though everyone else was in shirt sleeves. He had to hide the gun somewhere. Navy-blue trousers, tight across his thighs.

'Afternoon, Sergeant,' I said without stopping. 'Fancy meeting you here.'

He followed me down the stairs, sidestepping to avoid treading on a thin-armed young man sitting in the sun reading.

'Been to a wedding. Mickey Doolan's daughter. Thought I might browse the dudes. You never know what weddings and funerals might bring out of the woodwork.'

He drew level with me, pacing fast to keep up. 'Heard you had a bit of bother.'

'What bit of bother would that be?'

'Yesterday. Glebe. Able to leap temple walls in a single bound.'

'It was no bother, no bother at all. How did you get to hear about it?'

'It's usually quiet down that end of Glebe on a Sunday afternoon. Wasn't so quiet yesterday. Trying out for a part in *The Flying Nun?*'

Very funny, I thought, but I wasn't laughing. Not even smiling.

'What's it to you what I do with my Sunday afternoons?' I stood still now. We'd reached the quiet street where the Daimler was parked. I wasn't going to invite him in. He probably had a car parked in a No Standing zone anyway.

'Thought you might be on to some breakers.'

'The only place I'd be on breakers is Bondi.'

He laughed. Or rather, said, 'Ha, ha. Bank breakers. Thought maybe they were holed up in the temple. Religious asylum or something.'

'I'm sure if they'd been there you would have found them. Anyway, the matter is no longer of interest to me,' I said airily. 'I'm no longer looking.'

'You've found what you were looking for?' he asked suspiciously.

'Boredom set in.' I yawned. 'Like it is now. Good day, Sergeant.'

I parked the car in Queen Street, Woollahra, and walked into the gallery where the Chinese detective had shown me some of his six thousand years of civilisation.

The same girl was there and she recognised me. 'You are friend of James,' she said. That's debatable, I thought, but smiled just the same. 'James my friend too,' she said, with a hint of one-upmanship.

Then I noticed her earrings—diamonds in an antique gold setting, replicas of the ones he'd given me. Or maybe it was me who got the replicas. I stopped smiling.

'I would like to look at the cabinets,' I said to her, like a serious buyer.

'Cabinets?'

'Boxes.'

'Oh yes,' she beamed. 'You like boxes? This way, please.'

She took me to the same room and I looked at the same boxes. Looked at all of them, from every possible angle. Even picked one or two up and examined the bottom of them.

Searched in vain for that one small detail that had been missing from the photos in the Library.

The keyhole.

Not one of the boxes had a keyhole.

So what was the key all about and why was James Ho willing to trade six thousand years of civilisation for a detailed description of it?

I brought the photo of the key back to mind. Not the dragon but the intricate unlocking mechanism. The six teeth. Some short, some long.

They couldn't physically unlock a series of boxes with no keyhole.

But they might tell you how to do it.

This pebble created such ripples on the not so calm lake of my mind that I hardly noticed bumping into two people on my way out of the cabinet room.

Two people that I'd seen before. And in two separate places. A man and a woman.

As I bumped into him the man raised his walking-stick in a reflex action then relaxed it and smiled. His mouth was full of gold teeth. They were almost as intriguing as the badly botched skin graft on the side of his face. He pulled his black hat down to cover it and I saw again the same flashy gold ring he'd worn at the snooker room in Cabramatta.

The woman wore leather trousers. She flicked her hair back, the same gesture I'd seen in the lift at the Airport Hilton. I remembered then the destination she had given the cab driver.

Cabramatta.

And here they were together, the man in the black hat and James Ho's high-class prostitute. What a coincidence. Sydney was a small town. But I wouldn't want to draw a map of it.

It was just after two when I arrived at Brian Collier's office.

'You're lucky to catch me,' he said. 'I was about to go off for a late lunch.'

'Sounds like a great idea. Where are we going?'

'The Rose and Crown. You remember.'

Yes, I remembered. It was at the Rose and Crown that I'd met up with this man that I hadn't seen since childhood.

'You've got a lot of fans out there,' he said, handing me a box. It was full of letters. There must have been a hundred of them.

We ordered rare steaks and a couple of bottles of Cascade, and went to the same table by the window. Brian's table.

We'd hardly sat down when a young blond man wearing glasses came up. 'Brian Collier?' he asked nervously. Brian looked at him, neither affirming nor denying. 'Got a minute? I'd like to talk to you.' He looked at me then back to Brian. Brian still didn't answer. 'Later maybe,' said the young man. Brian nodded and went back to his drink.

'You never stop working in this game,' Brian said when he'd gone, 'not even at lunchtime.'

Our number was called and we went to the counter to pick up our steaks, adding condiments—mustard for me, tomato sauce and horseradish for Brian.

'I have one of these two, three times a week; and you know something? They're always perfect. How's yours?'

I swallowed the mouthful I was chewing. 'Perfect.'

'Aren't you going to open your mail?'

'You curious?'

'Moderately. News on the bank job is as dead as a doornail. You never know, there might be something of interest in that lot.'

He had a slightly more persuasive manner than Detective Sergeant Campbell, more open-handed, never overbearing. I told him about Campbell.

'Things must be quiet on that front too if they're watching the private detectives.' He put down his knife and fork and leaned on his elbow. 'You know, if those boys keep their mouths shut and don't get too cocky they're home and hosed.'

'The cops aren't going to learn anything more by watching me. I've taken myself off the case.'

Brian looked at me with eyebrows raised, more a query than surprise.

'The client was more trouble than the case.'

'Well, you won't be needing these then.' He'd called my bluff.

I picked up the box of letters and put them under my chair, between my feet.

'I did say discretion guaranteed. Don't want these doing the rounds of your office.'

'Is there anyone you trust?'

'Trust you. Don't trust your gossip columnists who might like to get their grubby little hands on them.'

'Why? Are you rich and famous?'

I laughed. 'The only way I'd get rich and famous is to rob a bank.'

I surprised myself. I knew how to do it now. If I had a few people on the team who knew about lift circuitry and thermo-lancing. Maybe I could do a Tech course.

'Let me know when you do, I'd like to be first cab off the rank.'

'Of course, Brian.'

'Well then,' he was already standing up and buttoning his jacket. 'I'd better get back in there and see who the crims are shooting.'

I picked up the box of letters and walked out with him.

'Any more lonely letters come in, I'll send them your way. I don't believe trouble with the client will stop you finishing what you started.' We stopped at the Daimler. 'How do you do it? There's never a parking spot when I want one.'

'Don't you watch TV? Private investigators always get a parking spot. Right outside the door.'

'See you round the traps, Claudia.'

The heat had stopped being stifling and was now merely monotonous. I got another bottle of Cascade from Jack and went upstairs. There were no nasty surprises waiting for me. Except Mrs Chen, on the Ansafone. She wanted me to contact her urgently. I put on Vince Jones and wondered how many times you had to play a tape before it wore out. Vince started crooning and I started going through my mail.

There was something impressive about getting all these letters at once. Till I started reading them. About thirty per cent were obscene and another thirty were boring. Lots of them were addressed to the Dragon Lady and signed St George. Very imaginative.

At the end of the first side of Vince I'd ploughed through at least seventy of them. Lots of pieces of straw in the haystack but no needles. I thought about what Collier had said, about them keeping quiet and not getting too cocky. But you'd want to tell someone. I was banking on that. And I hoped that someone was going to be me.

By the eighty-fifth letter I was still clutching at straws. I turned the tape back over but before it started playing the phone rang.

Steve. He had some results on the phone tap. There was one problem—it was in Chinese. But Steve said it sounded like quite a heated conversation. For Mrs Chen to sound heated the earth must have caved in.

'Can you bring them over tonight? We'll get Lucy to have a listen.'

Steve asked me if I wanted to continue with the tap. Off the case? Like hell I was. 'Yes.'

I went back to sifting through the letters. With letter ninety-two I struck gold.

Dear Dragon Lady,
A Happy New Year to you. Our little party did go off with a bang and was extremely rewarding. I am the person you describe in your ad. Fit, intelligent, with an explosive personality. It would be my pleasure to whisper sweet nothings in your ear. Be at St Mary's Cathedral, 3.15 p.m., 21 Feb. The confessional. I like single girls. If you are accompanied in any way there will be no meeting.

Yours in fellowship
Father John

I moved from the floor onto the bed. The letter had no particular distinguishing marks. It was laser printed on an A4 sheet, an ordinary quality you could buy by the ream. There were no spelling mistakes and nothing idiosyncratic, except the 'Father John'.

Now I got suspicious. Why had he replied? I told myself not to be so cynical; this was, after all, what I wanted. Maybe I could do something for him. Maybe, like me, it was sheer curiosity.

My first day off the case had produced more than all the days I'd spent on it. My chickens were coming home to roost. I felt quite pleased with myself. Tonight Lucy and Steve were coming over. We'd have a little party.

I went down to the shops to buy some party food.

'What a coincidence.'

It wasn't a coincidence, it was James Ho.

I sat on a stool with my shopping and asked Jack for a Corona. He opened it and stuck in a wedge of lemon. He'd never drink beer with lemon in it himself but he knew the trends and kept up with them. So did I. Selectively. You were never going to get me into a pair of those baggy shorts that were such a hit with every man, woman and child this summer.

'I heard you were at the gallery today.'

'News travels fast.'

'You wanted to make a purchase or just perusing?'

I wondered which of his women had told him; the girl at the gallery or the high-class prostitute. She certainly got around. But I wasn't going to give him the satisfaction of knowing I was more than just a little bit curious.

'How come that key you gave me was a lemon?'

'A lemon?'

'Oh come on, you were educated at Oxford, you know what a lemon is.'

'Would you like to sit down?' he enquired.

'I am sitting.'

'Not on a barstool. At a table. Where it's quieter.'

Jack gave me a passing glance as we walked away. He liked to keep his eye on things.

'OK, so tell me a story about the key.'

'It was time to give things a nudge,' he said simply. 'I wanted some action.'

'I don't know about you, but I got some. My room was ransacked over that key.'

He looked surprised.

'Don't tell me you didn't know. You seem to know everything else.'

'I'm sorry about your room. I expected you to give Mrs Chen the key.'

'Why did you give it to me in the first place? Why didn't you give it to her yourself?'

'You were employed to find the key. The key is your business.'

'And what's yours?'

'Mine is to find a set of boxes.'

'And whoever's got them is just going to hand them over to you?'

He smiled a winning smile. 'I don't expect it to be easy but I am prepared for that contingency. But first I have to ascertain whether the boxes contain holy relics.'

'And how are you going to do that?'

'By opening them.'

'And for that you need the key.'

'Would you like another drink?' he grinned.

I said no. I didn't want him leaving the table before I had a few more answers.

'Those boxes you showed me at the gallery didn't have key-holes.'

'And it took you only two visits to notice. You're very good, Ms Valentine.'

I tried to look unruffled. Not an easy job with clenched teeth. I was in no mood for sarcasm. This was not the first time the bastard had got the better of me

'Why don't you just try jemmying them open?'

'If they are what I think they are I don't want to damage them. Besides,' he said, lowering his already lowered voice, 'it may be very dangerous if they are not opened in the correct way.'

'Dragon breath going to come out and spread all over the palace, is it?'

'Sarcasm doesn't become you, Ms Valentine.'

'You've never complained before.' I took the wedge of lemon out of the Corona and sucked it. I liked the tart bitter taste. 'Do you know where the boxes are?'

'Not exactly.'

'Do you know who has them?'

'Perhaps.'

I put the sucked-out lemon in the ashtray and licked my lips.

'OK, let's try some yes and no answers. The people who have the boxes, are they putting pressure on Mrs Chen?'

'Yes.'

'For the key?'

He didn't have to tell me the answer to that.

'Why didn't Mrs Chen tell them the key was now out of reach? That it had gone in that bank robbery?'

'She is a very proud woman, as you have probably noticed. She would not like her enemies to think she was without her symbol of power. Besides,' he said, moving close to whisper in my ear, 'they had an ace that would make Mrs Chen show her hand.'

'Which is?'

He moved away quickly.

'Ah, good evening, Mr Angell.'

I turned around. Lucy and Steve were standing there. Steve with a bag full of equipment and looking none too happy.

'Not interrupting anything, am I?' he said sarcastically.

'Time for me to go,' said Ho. 'I'll be in touch.'

Steve watched him all the way to the door. His face resembled a thunderstorm.

'Drinks?' I suggested brightly, trying to steer him into fair weather.

'Yeah,' said Steve, 'I'll come with you.'

'What was that all about?' he said when we got to the bar.

'Just business.'

'Always is, isn't it?'

We returned to the safety of a third party—Lucy.

'He's the guy from Darling Harbour, isn't he?'

'Yes,' I said briefly. The less said about him at the moment the better.

'Mmm, even better close up, don't you think?'

'No,' I said.

'I see,' said Lucy, seeing something entirely different.

You could have cut the air with a knife.

'Well,' I said gaily, 'why don't we go upstairs and have a party? Got some edibles here and a bottle of Veuve Clicquot.' I was looking at Steve. He is rather partial to a drop of the widow. We'd spent our first night together with her. He forced a smile. It was going to be some party.

The edibles were all things you could just pop into your mouth—little curried pastries, sushi, carrot and celery sticks, slices of brie with sundried tomato wrapped in a basil leaf. This was Balmain after all.

Steve set up his tapes and we settled in to listen.

The first call was to Mrs Chen from the restaurant, telling her that I'd rung. The next one was mine to the house. I'd never heard my voice taped like that. A bit sibilant, but not too bad.

My own phone rang. We stopped the tape. It was Mrs Chen herself.

Steve stopped eating the brie and Lucy stopped eating the carrot sticks.

Mrs Chen started off with an apology, almost choking on the words, then asked if we could meet at the restaurant. Three o'clock tomorrow afternoon. I said I'd think about it.

'Well,' I said, after I'd hung up, 'let's keep this show rolling.'

Steve wiped his hands on his jeans and turned the tape back on. It was Mrs Chen's voice and a rather unpleasant male voice on the other end. Then a child's voice and Mrs Chen. Lucy was scribbling on her pad, an intent look on her face.

'Play it again, Steve,' she said.

He played it again.

'OK,' said Lucy, 'got it.'

Child: When are you going to come and visit?

Mrs Chen: Soon, Alice, soon. What are you doing?

Child: I'm doing drawing but I don't like it here. All they give me to eat is yukky noodles.

Man's voice: She will be eating noodles till you hand over the key.

Click. End of conversation.

But what I'd heard I found extremely interesting.

'Who's the child? A relative?'

Lucy shrugged her shoulders. 'She's got a few nieces. Don't know their names. I managed to avoid the intricacies of that generation of Chens.'

There was one more call, from Charles at the restaurant, to his mother at home. Lucy had a couple of goes at this one.

It was about me. Charles was telling his mother she had behaved like a one-legged monkey, that if she didn't want to go to the police, I was the only one who could help them. She said she would ask Kuan Yin for guidance.

End of tape.

The food was nearly all gone and so was the champagne. But it hadn't done the trick.

'Well, I'm off.' Lucy got up. 'It has been most entertaining. Let me know any further developments. And let me know if Cute Bum shows up again,' she added, giving me a nudge.

'I'll come with you,' said Steve.

'Steve?' My voice was full of question marks.

'I'll wait downstairs,' said Lucy, ducking out.

'Aren't you staying?' I asked, when Lucy had made herself scarce.

'Oh, you can slot me in this evening can you? Well I'm sorry, I've made other plans.' He didn't sound like he was sorry at all. 'I'm going to the Toucan Tango with Lucy.'

'But you don't like dancing,' I said, taken aback.

'I can always learn. I'm sure Lucy will make an excellent teacher. At least she's not so caught up with "business associates" as you seem to be. You do whatever you want to do, you see whoever you want to see, but as soon as you snap your fingers everyone has to jump. Well this time, Claudia, I'm not jumping.'

He slammed the door and was gone. I could feel my cheeks burning and my eyes brimming.

I was alone in my room again and this time I didn't particularly like it. Expecting everyone to fit into the slot I'd allocated them. Did I? What do you want me to do, Steve, sit sweetly on a cushion and bat my eyelids?

It was Ho, James Ho, who'd triggered off this outburst. Why did I feel so guilty?

I finished off the champagne and crawled into bed. Things would look better in the morning.

There was a girl's face in the window, calling out to me. I had to go back for her but my legs wouldn't move. There were iron bars, her hands reached out, imploring me. It was Amy, my loved one. I tried and tried to run but I couldn't get back to her.

I woke up, the pillows wet with sweat. It was 3 a.m. I got up and washed my face. Walked out onto the balcony. The street below was quiet. Somewhere out there in the city Steve slept. If he wasn't still out dancing with Lucy.

I stood there taking long slow breaths till my thoughts had calmed down. Three o'clock. I had remembered the time. It was the time I'd arranged to meet Mrs Chen. It was an appointment I was going to keep.

It was a cool grey day and the waters of Darling Harbour were greenish. There was no entertainment in Tumbalong Park and I wasn't followed. I walked on into Chinatown. Into the Red Dragon, straight up the stairs. No-one attempted to stop me.

Mrs Chen was sitting in her private office smoking a cigarette. Long, elegant and shaking in her hand. A pot of coffee stood waiting. I waved it away when she offered me some. She stood up and walked around the room a little. Went to the window and looked out. She came back and ashed an extremely long ash. She stubbed the cigarette out and it sat at a right angle in the ashtray. There were a few other butts in there as well, also half-smoked, also at right angles. She drew a breath and looked me in the eye.

'First I must apologise if my behaviour towards you has appeared less than. . .civilised.'

That was putting it mildly, but it was not the moment to say so.

'Mrs Chen,' I said softly, 'who's Alice?'

She put her hand to her forehead and massaged it.

'Alice is my granddaughter. Yes,' she said, seeing my reaction, 'Charles' daughter.' She lit another long elegant cigarette.

'Some years ago my son had a. . .liaison with a woman.' She cleared her throat. 'A prostitute. She blackmailed the family with the child. Normally I would not deal with a woman of her. . .position, but there was Alice. Perhaps I was foolish, I fell in love with the child. And I bought her. Gave the mother a substantial sum of money on the condition that she leave the country and never attempt to contact the child.'

'And now she has.'

Mrs Chen's brow furrowed. 'No, I do not think this is the case. I think others. . . Alice has been kidnapped.' That word was the trigger. Victoria Chen flopped back on the sofa. Tears started to work their way down her cheeks. When she'd had that first phone call she may have cried in shuddering sobs but now they were reduced to a thin steady stream.

'It is worse than death. To know the child is with strangers. Who may not treat her kindly. Who may kill her. It is like being in a box, a box just slightly bigger than your body, perhaps a coffin, with knives sticking out of the walls. You must move so little, so carefully. Any sudden movement and. . .'

She didn't have to go on. I knew already how it felt. My dream of Amy and my inability to move, how I would have cut my heart out if that would have saved her.

I was careful not to go to Mrs Chen and put a comforting arm around her. She did not invite that sort of contact.

'Who's got her, Mrs Chen?'

'Members of the Sun Yee On Tong. A Triad group.'

This was the most informative Mrs Chen had been throughout our acquaintanceship. I sat silent, waiting for her to continue.

'You are probably aware that the ethnic Chinese community in Australia is changing. Many new elements have entered the flow of newcomers to this country. And this country takes the bad with the good. Screening procedures are not very efficient.'

She paused. I took up the slack.

'Why are the Triads trying to get at you?'

'The Chen family is influential. We have the respect of the people, we do welfare work for the community, we do not turn away any reasonable request. Obviously, a powerful family attracts those who wish to grab some of that power rather than earning it.'

'Why are they holding Alice?'

'Her life in exchange for the key.'

'I think I know where Alice is,' I said. 'At the temple in Glebe.'

Mrs Chen sighed. 'She *was* at the temple. Sifu was looking after her, and Amah, her nanny. They were already threatening me. Alice is my jewel. I hid her there as a safety precaution till you found the key.'

Mrs Chen started pacing again. She came back to the table, lit another cigarette, and expelled a jet of smoke.

'Alice was forcibly taken from the temple on Sunday night. I don't know how they discovered where she was. Perhaps you do, Miss Valentine. I believe you visited the temple that day.'

She may not have been trying to implicate me but that was certainly the way I felt. Someone had followed me there that day and I'd been so busy following Mrs Chen's man I hadn't noticed. *You are a woman. You are invisible.* I hadn't been invisible on the streets of Glebe that day. I felt sick.

I poured myself some coffee and swallowed its bitterness like some sort of penance.

'What's so special about the key that they are willing to go to these lengths to get it?'

'The key is a symbol of power for the Chen family. Without it we are like Samson without his hair. Without the key the Sun Yee On could squeeze us out of Chinatown just like that.' Her fingers curled inwards and made a fist. 'The key is passed from father to eldest son but Charles. . .' she pursed her lips, 'Charles does not have the strength of his father. He is not yet ready to become the keeper of the key. In the meantime, its power is invested in me.'

'What is its particular power?'

She was on the edge, afraid to take the final step, as if the words themselves might make the thing happen.

'The key opens boxes, doesn't it?' I said.

She bowed her head in a slow, deliberate movement.

'Yes,' she said slowly, 'I believe that is part of the power of the key.'

She poured two more coffees and offered me one. This time I

didn't refuse. I held the cup in my hand. So small, so delicate, if you didn't handle it carefully it would smash to pieces.

Mrs Chen rested a spoonful of sugar on the surface of the coffee and we both watched it slowly turn brown. Brown sugar, the sweet sickly taste. Brown sugar, the sweet sickly smoke hitting the back of your throat.

I watched her slowly take a sip.

'The boxes are a symbol of power for the Sun Yee On Tong. They are believed to contain great treasure. For centuries the key and the boxes have been separated. So that the power is divided. Now the Tong has moved into Australia. If the leader were to possess the key he would have everything, the Chen power as well.'

She looked up at me and held my gaze. 'For Alice I would give up the key.'

Her voice was barely above a whisper, as if it was coming from a place deep within her.

'You realise,' I said just as softly, 'that the key may well be irretrievable. They may have dumped it, had it scrapped.'

'No, Miss Valentine, the key exists and it must be found. There is no alternative.'

This was the sort of attitude that built empires, but for want of a nail empires were lost.

'I will pay any amount of money for its safe return.'

'There are some things even your money won't buy. Perhaps it is time to bring in the police.'

Mrs Chen's body clenched as tight as the fist she'd made a few moments ago. 'I was not to inform the police about this matter. If they suspect police they will kill Alice.'

'Do you really think that once they have the key they will simply hand Alice over?'

It was the hope that all parents have, that their child in danger will be returned safely, that its disappearance is a moment out of time, that once the child is returned clocks will start ticking again, steady as a heart beat.

'They must.'

I looked at Mrs Chen's face, the one she wanted me to see,

and the other. The one that moved when she moved, that stayed still when she did, that disappeared if you looked at it full on. The shadow that was tacked onto her like a secret. *A prominent and respected businessman in Sydney's Chinatown.* It was not businessman, it was businesswoman.

The Dragonhead of the Chinatown Triad was Mrs Chen.

I got up and walked over to the window. Down below in the street life strolled by. The life that Mrs Chen controlled. The life built on the dragon's back. The life that was in danger of falling off when the dragon woke from her sleep, that would burn in her breath.

Mrs Chen and the leader of the other Tong; two Dragonheads vying for the pearl of prosperity.

When I came back from the window I saw not the Dragonhead but a woman in distress, a woman who feared for the life of the child she loved.

Finding one small child in this city would be the same as trying to find the key. A needle in a haystack. But there was much more at stake now. And I wasn't just doing a job anymore. I was implicated: I was the one who had led them to Alice.

'Do you have any idea where they might be keeping her?'

Mrs Chen's eyebrows moved together like two neat tadpoles. 'She is not here in Chinatown. I would know if it was Chinatown.'

I looked at her. Briefly this time. Nothing moves in Chinatown without you swatting it, does it Mrs Chen? But something is moving, shifting; empires are not eternal. And empresses can't rule without their symbols of power.

'Next time they let Alice talk to you, listen for background sound, ask her what the room is like, what she can see out of the window. Maybe they'll let her send you a drawing. Keep up the communication as long as possible.'

'You will find the key, Miss Valentine?'

I thought of the meeting at St Mary's. It was a long shot and I didn't want to raise Mrs Chen's hopes.

'I'll do my best.'

I was too close to the hospital to pass up the opportunity. I thought of phoning first, but the occasion warranted a personal appearance. It was late in the day. I hoped I'd catch Steve before he left.

To my dismay the clinic was still in session and there were quite a few people waiting. I started to head off again.

''Ere ya, love,' said a chap in a red and blue check flannel shirt, whose strings of hair had been plastered across his bald patch. He was patting an empty spot beside him on the bench. I hesitated. And was lost. I sat down. He stuck an elbow in my ribs. ''Ow long 'ave you 'ad yours done?'

'I haven't,' I said. 'How's yours keeping up?'

'Like a bloody bewdy. That Dr Angell's orright.' I refrained from telling him Steve wasn't a doctor; it might have given him another heart attack. 'Ya know the funny thing about it?' He didn't wait for an answer. 'The medication. The bloody medication. A nip of whisky before meals. Doctor's orders!' he beamed.

'Well, don't overdo it,' I said. 'Keep it down to a nip.'

The door to Steve's office opened. There were voices and an elderly gent appeared. He nodded his head in a final goodbye. Then Steve appeared, hands casually in the pockets of his hospital jacket. His eyes scanned the faces in the waiting room, alighting briefly on mine. His smile set for a moment, a slight tensing of muscles, then he moved on. 'Mr McCarty?'

The gent in the blue and red flannel shirt stood up as if he'd been picked out of a television audience for a special prize.

Steve made no other acknowledgement of my presence there.

It had been a mistake to come in the first place. How would I feel if he'd turned up while I was on the job? My cheeks flushed hot; it felt like there were ants crawling round inside them. I stood up again.

'I'll see you in a minute, Ms Valentine,' he said. Then more quietly, 'Patience was never one of your virtues.'

I sat down. No-one talked to me. I stuck my head in a magazine and waited.

'Got a problem with your heart?'

I sat there and he stood, the air thick between us.

'I want to talk,' I said.

'Always what you want, eh Claudia?'

I breathed heavily, tightening my lips.

'Well,' he said, after a while, 'are you coming into my office or do you want to thrash this out in public?'

I chose the office.

'Look, whatever it is, I want...I'd like us to sort it out. I'd like to...open negotiations.'

'So, open.' He wasn't being very helpful and there was still tension in his voice.

'How do you feel?'

He leaned back in his chair and put his hands behind his head.

'Look, I'm a pretty easygoing guy but I'm not going to jump through a hoop every time you snap your fingers.'

'What is it?' I said softly. 'Aren't I saying "please" and "thank you" enough?'

He shifted position, leaning forward now. 'Something like that. You're not the sort of person to pussyfoot around; you ask straight questions and you like straight answers. OK, so things are tough out there, your job is tough.' He leaned further towards me. 'But it doesn't have to be tough in here with me, Claudia.'

'I know, I know, the toughness is an occupational hazard. Sometimes I forget to turn it off.'

I didn't expect happily-ever-after from Steve, I didn't expect it from anyone. In the dark night all you had was yourself but it was nice, more than nice, to know there was another human being there and that you could rest easy with him. Have the boundaries disappear if only for a little while.

But what I was doing was more than just a job. I'd moulded myself into it, it had become part of me, part of being myself, of taking action in the world. Not sitting at home and hearing about the world from someone else. I didn't believe I had to make a choice at this moment; I didn't believe this was a showdown, merely an impasse.

'I know all that,' said Steve. 'I live with it. Not all the time, just occasionally, but lately the occasionally has become too frequent.'

'Would you rather I didn't involve you in my work?'

He smiled. 'No, not really. It sure beats the hell out of checking these old geezers' pacemakers in the excitement stakes. But why does Charlie Chan have to be in on everything?'

'Charles Chen?' It took me a minute to realise he meant James Ho.

My old mate James Ho. All that stuff about snapping my fingers may have been true but that's not what was needling Steve. It was James Ho.

'He's in it, and has been since the beginning, since before the beginning maybe. But I didn't ask him in and it wasn't him I asked to bug Mrs Chen, it was you. Lucy must have told you he was nosing around in Chinatown. Did she say anything about him the other night?'

'Nothing you'd like to hear. She's a little concerned about you poking your nose in Mrs Chen's business.'

'Why?'

'Big wheel in Chinatown. Rolls right over some people.'

'Her granddaughter's been kidnapped. I don't care about the rest.'

We were back to talking about business again.

'Heard anything interesting on the phone?' As soon as it had blundered out of my mouth I knew it had been the wrong thing to say.

'I've been doing my job all day, not yours. And I'm still doing it. I'll give you a call sometime,' he said, dismissing me.

I closed the door behind me and didn't turn around. I walked down the stairs and out into the street. The setting sun was splashing colour in the sky. Bright, far too bright for how I was feeling.

There was a snarl of traffic at White Bay but once I turned off the Crescent it eased up. I drove along Federal Street skirting the now black waters of Rozelle Bay. The other side was park and there wasn't anyone about except a man walking his greyhounds. I turned right, entering the leafy streets of large houses and pulled up alongside the brick wall of the temple grounds.

The gates that had been open on my first visit were now shut, the green lions guarding them. There was a buzzer by one of the lions. I pressed it, announced myself, and heard a click.

The big camphor laurel cast shadow on the lawn that was now fully mown. It looked like a snowfield. Not white though, shades of grey. There was a light on in the office and up the back behind the banana palms a dull orange glow, perhaps the light from a kerosene lamp.

Standing like a sentinel at the doorway was the monk in the maroon robes.

'I am here on behalf of Mrs Chen.'

He nodded acknowledgement. 'Would you like tea?'

This might take some time but I guessed that's how things went at the temple. I might also learn some patience, I thought ruefully. I was in no hurry. I had all night if necessary.

The tea had been stewing on the stove but it didn't taste bitter.

'Would you like to sit down?' he invited.

It looked like a physical impossibility in there, even on the floor.

He flicked a switch and a light went on outside near the tables and chairs. We went out. A few insects hovered round the light while others dive-bombed like kamikaze pilots.

The girl had been taken in the early hours of Monday morning, the morning after I had visited the temple. She was there at midnight and when he'd checked again at six she was gone.

Was he the only other person on the premises?

No. A woman who worked for Mrs Chen had been asleep in the same room as the girl but she had not woken. I asked for her name. He said Mrs Chen would tell me.

'What about the boy up the back?' He looked at me silently. 'The boy who sleeps under the tarpaulin.'

'He is the gardener; he stays here sometimes.'

Sometimes must have been fairly often. He was here on my first visit and I was pretty sure he was up there now.

'I'd like to talk to him.'

'Wait one moment. I will see if he is here.'

Who else would it be burning a kerosene lamp up there? Maybe he was going through some sort of rites of passage, pretending he was in the wilderness, fending off wild mosquitoes among the banana palms.

Sifu walked into the night garden.

When he was around the corner of the building I walked in the same direction. I stood at the edge of the path watching. The lamp went out then there was some dark movement up there. I walked up to where the light had been. I saw a shadow coming towards me. Sifu.

Then I saw another. Climbing over the back wall.

I sprinted up there and scaled the wall.

On the other side the boy was running down the street, shirt-tails flying. I started running after him. He heard my footsteps and looked back for a second. I gained a few steps on him. He ran around the corner. I got to the corner in time to see him fling open the door of an orange Kombivan. I reached him before he had time to close the door. He swung his feet out to kick me away. I blocked his legs with my forearm and swept them up so that he did a clumsy sort of somersault in the front seat. I took the keys out of the ignition and threw them out onto the street.

He smelled like a wet puppy and was looking at me with huge eyes.

I said, 'I'm not going to bite you. I probably won't even bark. Where are you off to in such a hurry?'

He didn't answer, merely sat there with his lips pursed as if I was about to try and prise them open to get the information. In the streetlight I could see the sweat glistening on him. I watched the hands and feet carefully but he didn't really look like he was going to move them in my direction.

'I put in a polite request to speak to you and you not so politely jumped over the fence,' I said, in soft you-can-trust-me tones. 'Just what did that man say to you?'

'He's not "that man", he's Sifu. The Master.' He said it like a truculent child.

'OK. Sifu.' I said it like a sigh.

'He said you were a cop and that you wanted to talk to me.'

'One out of two. I want to talk to you but I'm not a cop.'

'What do you want to know?' he said, looking into his lap.

'Considering the circumstances perhaps we can start with what you don't want me to know. What you had to run away from.'

Silence filled the van.

I gave him a mental nudge and repeated, 'I'm not a cop.'

He remained sullen. He didn't look old enough to have a driver's licence. That didn't mean he couldn't drive though.

'How old are you?'

'Eighteen.'

'Can I see your driver's licence?'

'I don't have it on me.'

'Rego papers?'

He stuck out his bottom lip.

'Doesn't matter, I can check it.'

'Why would you want to?' He looked startled.

'Why would you not want me to?'

The silence came in like a tide.

'Perhaps we should go back and talk with Sifu. You might feel more comfortable in his company.'

He sat with a sulky look on his face.

'What do you do at the temple?'

'I garden. And,' he added more reluctantly, 'I am a pupil of Sifu. I am learning the Way.'

'Do you live there, up among the banana palms?'

'Sort of.'

'It's a nice spot. Doesn't it get cold in winter?'

'I haven't been there in winter.'

'What do your parents think of you living here?'

I'd finally put my finger on the trigger.

'They don't know.'

'And I guess they wouldn't like it, eh? They'd worry you didn't have clean underwear, enough warm jumpers.'

He smiled for the first time. The teeth were yellowish.

'Don't worry, I won't dob you in.' I felt like I was down the back of the school toilets having a smoke.

'Did you know the little girl who was staying here?'

'Alice? Yeah, she was my little mate, used to help me with the weeding and stuff.'

'What happened to her?'

'She went back to her uncle's.'

'Where does he live?'

He shrugged his shoulders. 'One day she just wasn't there.'

'Were you here that night? The night before she. . . left?'

'I've been here for the last three months, every night.'

'Did you notice anything that night? Noises?'

He shrugged again. 'Why should I? Sifu sometimes has visitors. I don't know. I look after myself up there.'

'Did he have any visitors that night?'

He thought about it. 'Don't think so. Don't remember.'

'What do you do up there by yourself at night?'

'I study mostly, meditate.'

'What were you doing that night?'

'Probably the same.'

'Do you think you can be more definite? It was only a week ago. Sunday night. The day visitors come.'

'I usually make myself scarce when they're around; it's all families and kids, you know the scene.'

I hadn't heard that phrase for years. On a religious trip, living out in the jungle in the middle of the inner city, maybe someone ought to preserve this guy as part of the National Heritage.

'And that night?'

'Well, they all go about sunset; that's usually when I come back. I don't have lessons with Sifu on Sundays. So, up to my shack, do a bit of reading.'

'You weren't out all of that day. I saw you, asleep in your shack.'

'Maybe. In the afternoon there's not so many people about. They come in the morning. Offer prayers, have a cup of tea and a chat, the kids play around.'

'Did Alice play with the kids?'

'No, she stayed in her room when there were other people around.'

'Did you ever wonder about that?'

'No.' His response was genuine. I suppose when you are on the Way you don't ask questions, you just accept the Master's wisdom, when and if he decides to drop a pearl of it on you. Like Inspector Clouseau, you never know where the next lesson is coming from.

'What was she like?'

'Quiet, serious. She didn't play much outside and when she did the old woman kept watch over her, even when we were weeding the garden.' He looked at me with those child's eyes. 'She was in trouble, wasn't she?'

'Yes. Do you know why she was being kept here?'

'Buddhists don't question their life, they accept it, detach themselves from it.'

I hoped he wasn't going to start preaching.

'You mentioned an old woman. Who was she?'

'She watched the child. Just sat there, watched.'

'Where did she stay?'

'In the temple. In Alice's room.'

'Where is she now?'

'She left.'

I'd gone as far as I could with him. 'Want to go back?'

We got out of the van. I picked up the keys and handed them to him. He didn't drive off, he came back.

Sifu was still waiting at the tables beneath the camphor laurel.

'Sifu,' I said respectfully, 'may I see the child's room?'

It was upstairs. The window that had framed her face so precisely was opposite the door. There were two narrow beds. There was no other furniture apart from a bedside cupboard with a shrine on top of it. The place was clean. I wondered if it had been Sifu who was so meticulous with this room while his office remained a mess.

'Has the room been cleaned since. . . ?'

His head moved diagonally, almost from side to side, the movement which in the East signifies yes, but which looks like no to western eyes.

'It is a guest room.' As if he was expecting more children to be brought to the sanctuary of the temple. For Alice that sanctuary had been only temporary.

'Yet you left the offerings.'

There was an orange cut into segments and some little crawling critters anxious to be offered to Buddha, or perhaps anxious only to suck the sweet juices and turn them into vinegar. The floor of the shrine was powdery with incense ash and wafted up the smell of what was once sandalwood.

I opened the drawer of the bedside cupboard. It was full of messages written on thin strips of paper. Fortune cookie messages, some of them run-of-the-mill printed ones, others handwritten from Grandma to Alice. They weren't messages anymore, just scraps of paper.

On the wall were child's drawings. They were done in Texta pens. She had a good eye for detail.

Sifu brushed the crawly things off the fruit.

'Where are her Textas?' He looked at me blankly. 'Pens—for drawing. Did she take them with her?'

'I did not find drawing pens.'

They had let her take them? To keep the child quiet? Maybe the kidnappers were kindly. But I didn't like her chances.

I looked under the bed, an area that men seldom clean, not even Masters. There was a pink object like a bent sausage, and lots of dust. I reached my hand in and felt something cold and mildly clammy. I brought it out to the light. It was a doll's arm. But there wasn't a one-armed doll in the room that I could see.

'She had a doll?'

'Yes.'

'Where is it?'

He didn't know. So the child took with her the doll and the Texta pens. It must have been some comfort to her. I could do with a bit of comfort myself.

Mrs Chen looked almost pleased to see me. Hopeful yet apprehensive. I knew how she felt.

'The old woman that was looking after Alice. I'd like to talk to her.'

'Her English is not good.'

'I'm sure you'll help out, Mrs Chen.'

She smiled. There was relief in that gesture. 'I have questioned her myself.'

'I'm sure you have, but I might ask different questions.'

She went away. I looked out at the Daimler on the gravel and thought about the first time I'd come here to the Chen mansion. It didn't feel anywhere near so opulent now.

Mrs Chen came back with a woman slowly but surely shuffling behind her. She must have been a hundred. She was wearing a grey silk pants suit with little black motifs on it. Her feet were remarkably small.

'This is Amah.'

The woman looked at me with bright beady eyes. Eyes that looked like they wouldn't miss a trick.

It didn't take me long to realise that Mrs Chen was right about her English. She was limited to 'hello' and 'how are you?'. We couldn't carry on a conversation without Mrs Chen's intervention.

'What's the story so far?'

'She says she was knocked out.'

'Any damage?' She looked like even a light tap to the head would be enough to send her permanently to nirvana.

'Nothing that is visible. There are ways of doing it that don't leave a trace.' I looked at Mrs Chen. Once again I saw the Dragonhead.

'Did she see them? Before they knocked her out?'

'No. She was sleeping; they hardly disturbed the bed.'

They must have been quiet. Quiet as thieves in the night. Old ladies are light sleepers, particularly when on the alert for the night sounds of a child.

So I didn't have a witness. Either she was lying or the kidnappers had been very careful.

'Ask her about the doll,' I said.

Apparently the child slept with it.

'Was it there after Alice disappeared?'

No.

'What about the Texta pens?'

She didn't know. She didn't look in the drawers. She was only concerned about one thing missing from the room. The child.

Though it was Mrs Chen doing most of the answering I directed my questions each time to Amah, looking at her eyes, for any flicker, for something the words might not tell me. I looked and I listened. But the kidnappers made sure she had no story to tell. I talked to the old woman some more but she had nothing to add to the picture.

I drove back to the city and home via Chinatown. Slowly.

A wind had come up and a few pieces of garbage gusted into the air like paper birds. People winced in the wind, thrusting their hands in their pockets and hunching their heads down low in their collars; others confronted it head on. But mostly the streets of Chinatown were empty. I looked for Alice. Hoping. Knowing she wouldn't be there.

Wind was the worst sort of weather for the city. Under the sun the harbour sparkled and in the rain, well, that grey rain is what cities are about. But the wind blows up the canyons of the streets, blowing the city's grit into your face.

I kept the car window open. I always have it open unless there are hailstones pounding in.

I was crossing the upward curve of the flyover to my part of the city. Not in Chinatown. Where would you hide a Chinese kid? Among other Chinese. Cabramatta. It was a long shot but I had to start somewhere and no other road looked like it was going to lead anywhere promising. But as I knew from my first visit I stuck out like a sore thumb in Cabramatta.

It had to be someone who could blend in with the scenery. Who was more invisible than I had proved to be.

As far as I could see there was only one candidate.

When I got home I rang the Airport Hilton. I described James Ho to them. They told me there were a number of Asians staying who answered that description. In Italian kung fu shoes? They told me they never looked at their guests' feet. They hung up pretty quickly after that.

It was probably just as well. I had the feeling James Ho knew a whole lot more about this matter than he was telling me.

I had a quiet Scotch. I closed the french doors against the wind and lay on the bed. I was there to clear my mind and watch the thoughts floating across the still lake. There was plenty for me to think about alone in that bed. For a start there was Steve. Those thoughts crept in like unwelcome guests. I let them drift on, out of my line of vision. I closed my eyes, softly, slowly, and sent the relaxed movement of the eyelids through the entire body. I pictured Alice, the image of her framed in the window. I held it there and pulled it across the boundary into sleep.

It seemed a strange thing to do but it had a sense of urgency. I had to talk to Charles. Who'd been kept out of the limelight. Outshone by the powerful number of watts emanating from his mother. Then it became less strange; he was, after all, the child's father.

I rang the Chen residence. The phone was answered immediately. I identified myself and stated my purpose.

When Charles came to the phone he asked if I wouldn't rather talk to his mother. I told him I'd done that already. Several times. He didn't know if he could be of much help. I didn't know either but it was worth a try.

I was going to the Chen residence so frequently lately that I wondered whether it wouldn't be more convenient to rent a room there. The hired hands even smiled at me now.

Charles and I sat in the room with the heavy red curtains.

'Your mother not here?'

'No.' That was just the way I wanted it. I wanted to hear Charles' story, without his mother there putting words in his mouth. 'She's at the restaurant, in case the phone there...'

'Have you had any more calls?'

'No.'

'Didn't they say they were going to ring? Didn't you have an ultimatum?'

'Friday. The key must be returned by Friday.'

'Not a lot of time, is it? There's a faint possibility but...We should think of alternative ways to...extricate Alice.'

Extricate—to remove or free from complication, hindrance or difficulty; disentangle.

I had the feeling that life for Alice would never be free of those things, even if she was returned to the Chens.

'Can we have a cup of coffee, Charles?'

He looked startled. 'Coffee? Yes, coffee...I'm sorry I...' He'd forgotten his manners. He pressed a buzzer and the girl dressed like a French maid appeared. He said something to her in Chinese, she did a sort of a bow and went away.

'Cigarette?' he said, offering me a lacquer cigarette case with gold hinges.

'No, thank you,' I said politely.

He lit one for himself and put the case back into the pocket of a light linen jacket. The sleeves were pushed up and his arms were smooth and creamy. I couldn't see any needle marks.

'How close were you to Alice?'

He stared at the tip of his cigarette, as if wanting to avoid the question.

'I don't know,' he began, 'she...' He flicked the ash of the cigarette nervously, still not looking up. 'I liked her, she...she was more like a baby sister than my...' His eyes flashed up at me. 'You must understand, I was only seventeen!' he blurted out. 'A mistake of my youth,' he said more quietly.

I thought of my own kids, and the mistakes of my youth. Maybe they had come too soon but once they were there they were loved.

They were still loved.

The coffee arrived. The maid looked at Charles quizzically but he hardly acknowledged her presence. She left.

'Tell me about it,' I said, stirring my coffee.

'About what?'

'About Alice, about her mother.'

He sighed. 'I suppose it was a rebellion against my mother. My first, and she made sure it was my last,' he said, curling his lip. 'I knew she was a prostitute. Maybe I was in love with Tai May, maybe it was just because she was my first lover. She was still working when she got pregnant. She'd been brought to

Australia under false pretences, promised a job. Well, that was the job.'

'Who brought her here?'

'Men about town. Men who ran the racket, rich men, others who wanted to get rich. I wanted to marry her.' He laughed, more of a snort than a laugh. 'My mother of course wouldn't hear of it.' I could well imagine. 'She kept the child and sent the mother back. I never saw Tai May again. My mother thought it was better for me not to have contact.'

'How come the girl got pregnant? Prostitutes don't usually. They would have told her how to avoid it. Bad for business if she gets pregnant.'

'My mother said she did it deliberately, wanted to use our family, to marry our money.'

'She didn't marry it but she got the money anyway,' I observed.

'But not her child. That was my mother's way of punishing her.'

Mrs Chen was looking less and less likely to win any awards for Parent of the Year.

'And me,' he said quietly.

'Pardon?'

'And me!' he said, this time loud enough for the whole house to hear. 'Alice was my mother's way of punishing me. A living reminder of my mistake. Whenever I did anything without her approval she'd always remind me of Alice, of the trouble, the scandal I'd brought to the family. Some scandal,' he snorted. 'She always passed her off to the outside world as her niece. That, Miss Valentine, is my mother.'

'Why do you stay, Charles?' I asked softly.

'She's my mother.'

'That's not good enough, Charles.'

'She's a powerful woman. She could make things very difficult for me.'

'All you have to do is pack up your things and walk out that door.'

He smiled sheepishly. 'Easier said than done,' he pointed out.

I knew that. But I had done it and so had Lucy. It wasn't easy but neither was it impossible.

But I didn't belong to a powerful family. I suppose in this case it was a bit like asking Prince Charles why he didn't leave the Queen. It must be a real strain when the person you're grooming for power turns out to be a wimp.

I also had the feeling that if Charles proved a liability Mrs Chen could well arrange ways of getting rid of him.

'How much do you want your daughter back?'

'Before, I didn't...' He kneaded the veins standing out on the back of his hand. 'This crisis...' He steadied his hands on his knees. 'Now that Alice's life is in danger I realise how much she means to me.'

'And your mother?'

'I never really understood why she wanted Alice. She wanted to punish Tai May for what she felt she'd done to our family but it was more than that.' He took out another cigarette, lit it, then put the case on the table, among an assortment of gold ornaments. I never could understand this predilection for gold, far too gaudy for my taste. 'You know, they used to sell girl children in the land of my forefathers. And my mother wanted to keep this girl child, bring her up as her own.' He smiled wryly. 'My mother is...idiosyncratic. Sometimes she will do things that seem out of character, that no-one can explain. I think she saw strength in Alice, strength that perhaps she would have wanted in me.' He lowered his head.

I looked at him steadily. It takes a certain kind of strength to admit weakness.

'My mother's greatest wish is for Alice to replace her as...'

'Dragonhead.'

He looked up at me. 'Yes.'

'Well kidnapping is certainly going to toughen Alice up. Where do you think she is?'

'Cabramatta.'

My heart missed a beat, like he'd named a secret thing.

'Those hoods making trouble in our restaurant, they are Sun Yee On street-fighters. They make trouble in Cabramatta too.

Use it as their base. Now they are trying to move in on Chinatown.'

'Tell me about the key.'

He laughed. 'The key! My mother thinks it gives us power, but that power has been turned against us. My father was killed over it and now Alice is gone. Some old Chinese superstition about it being the key to great treasure. Well let them have their treasure. The Red Dragon restaurant and the other family properties aren't going to suddenly disappear overnight if we don't have the key. The people my mother looks after don't even know the key exists.'

Looks after. He made extortion sound like an act of charity.

I had always wondered what it was like for people like the Chens. They had so much to lose. But I wasn't trying to prop up an empire, I was trying to save the life of a child no matter which family she belonged to. I sat there thinking about the Chens I knew—the mother, the son, the granddaughter. A father who hadn't cared enough, a grandmother who cared too much.

All the wheeling and dealing in the city, all the dramas—the biggest ones occurred right here at the centre of things, in the family.

That key might have lost its charm as far as Charles was concerned but it still might be able to charm the people who had Alice.

St Marys Cathedral stood at a busy intersection where four roads converged. In nearby Hyde Park a flock of seagulls floated above the open lawn like scraps of paper caught up in the breeze. Shooting the breeze, for the sheer hell of it. There was a park bench conveniently placed directly opposite the front entrance to the cathedral. I'd arrived early, early enough to watch the comings and goings, early enough perhaps to see a man enter wearing size nine shoes. I don't know why I'd taken so much time over dressing; it wasn't like I was going on a date.

But it was a special occasion. I had on a soft black leather jacket, slim black trousers and black boots. My hair was up in combs and on top of it was a green hat. I thought I looked the business.

The thing I noticed about that towering facade was how relatively small the doors were. Easier for a camel to pass through the eye of a needle. Cars came and went as the lights changed from red to green then back again. Clouds raced eastwards behind the twin towers of the facade. I looked up at them because everything about the cathedral was designed to lift the eye heavenward. There were pointed archways, meeting like fingertips in prayer, above the doors. There was a huge rose window in the centre and cutting into the sky a cross. All around the cathedral was a spiked fence. With its turrets and buttresses it looked more like a fortress than a place of worship.

It also looked as though there'd be a lot of good hiding places inside.

I crossed the road and walked up the wide front steps. I decided not to go in through the front doors but through a less conspicuous entrance. I walked around the eastern side of the cathedral, overlooking a construction site with aluminium portables. Three engineers in white hard hats were standing in a huddle, talking almost mouth to ear to be heard above the sounds of construction.

I went into the cathedral through a small side door and immediately all sound was subdued. A dull amber light filtered down from the yellow glass high up in the walls.

Suddenly the cathedral was full of light, as if someone had turned up the dimmer switch. My first thought was that a miracle was about to happen. *Fiat lux*. Then I realised it was the sun coming in and out of the clouds. The fluctuation of light was to occur several times. It was very windy outside.

The rose window and other stained glass had lots of rich reds and blues in it. Christ with a bright red halo, bearing his cross, surrounded by supplicants in rich indigo. There were flashes of white light too from the cameras of Japanese tourists.

Behind the row of candles at the side altar was the Christian queen of heaven, complete with crown above her robes. She'd come a long way for a carpenter's wife of dubious pregnancy. A long way from Nazareth.

I started wandering now. I had plenty of time, looking more at the people than the architecture, looking for Father John. A schoolteacher came by with a flock of Asian children in tow, all wearing bottle-green tracksuits with gold stripes down the sleeves and the sides of the pants.

Being unaccustomed to Catholic churches, especially cathedrals, it took me a little time to locate the confessionals. There was a set of red cushioned doors that looked likely candidates but proved merely to be double doors to the outside world.

It was not until I got to the main entrance that I saw the Special Notices that gave the times of guided tours, masses and confession. In that order.

There were no confessions scheduled for 3.15.

There were quite a few confessionals on the western side of the cathedral. They were all locked but there was a clear panel rather like a mailbox slot in the frosted glass of each door. I looked in. Nothing but empty chairs.

It was 3.12. I had been in the cathedral twenty-five minutes. I had seen tourists, parties of schoolchildren, the odd individual at prayer. I had not seen a priest. Especially not one wearing size nine shoes.

Above the confessionals on the eastern side a light shone. A single yellow light above the middle door. It was open for business, an unscheduled confession.

A special confession, for me alone.

I patted my hair, adjusted my hat. I took a deep breath and walked to my rendezvous with destiny.

As I approached, my eyes were focused on the clear glass panel. But no matter how much I peered I couldn't see in. The panel had been blocked by a book. The Holy Bible.

I entered the adjacent box.

'Bless me Father, I haven't sinned but I believe you have.'

He chuckled. The throaty chuckle of someone who was enjoying himself.

'Keep talking,' he said.

'I believe you may recently have come into a large sum of money.'

'God helps those who help themselves.' He didn't sound like the punks who'd come up to me in the pub. His voice was muffled, and it wasn't just the partition between us. But it sounded rich, almost melodious. The voice of a man with a great deal of job satisfaction.

'I believe you *have* helped yourself.'

He didn't have anything to say to that.

'Do you wear size nine shoes?'

'I am an average man.'

'I believe you are more than average, you have knowledge of specialised subjects.'

'And so apparently do you.'

'It's my job to know.'

'So I've been told. I have been doing my own investigations.'

So he'd checked me out. And I'd come up smelling of roses.

'There are many people who would like to be having this

conversation with you. I'm curious as to why I'm the lucky one.'

'I like your style.'

'I think I like yours.'

'And your discretion. Guaranteed.'

'I am as good as my word. What exactly was it that appealed to you about my ad?'

'You understood. The urge to confess.'

Not quite.

He wanted to tell all right, but it wasn't the urge to confess, it was the urge to brag. It was not 'Bless me Father for I have sinned', it was 'Bless me Father because I am the smartest bastard in the world'.

'You chose the right place.'

'I know.'

'So let's hear it.'

He chuckled. 'It's not that simple and I'm not that foolish. You will notice that nothing specific has been said, nor will it, nothing that will stand up in court, nothing that will identify me.'

'This conversation will never get to court; it's strictly between you and me.'

'That's what I was banking on.'

'I like your choice of words.'

There was a pause. 'It was good, wasn't it.'

'It was brilliant,' I said.

I could almost feel the contentment. He was ready to tell me now.

'Was it the way the papers said?'

'Almost, but not quite. We did get in through the fourth floor window then go down to the basement. We did blast through the safes the way they said. What we didn't do was go out to nearby pubs. We stayed in the bank the whole time. Even when the alarm went off. Do you know what that's like? What nerve it takes? Not to run when you hear the alarm? To stay there, when all your instincts are telling you to get out? And the second time, when the guard came down to the basement. Hearing the lift door open, the light switched on. If only he'd looked further, if he'd removed the cardboard boxes we'd piled up. What if he had been clumsy and accidentally knocked them, or been a little more curious. But he wasn't. We weren't lucky, we were blessed.'

In my mind I could see him going over it all again, as he must have many times, smiling inwardly with satisfaction.

'Can we expect any repeat performances?'

'Not from us. Do it clean then disappear. I have resumed my normal life. When the time is right I will reap the fruits of my harvest.'

'Talking about harvest, I was interested in one particular fruit—a golden one, with a dragon on it.'

'Ah yes, there were many trinkets.'

I wondered how the Chens would feel hearing their key to power described as a trinket.

'Most of the items are no longer with us. We dumped a lot of those trinkets.'

'Dumped?'

'Too hard to get rid of, too identifiable. We dumped them in the harbour.'

My heart sank, right down to those depths. It was no longer a question of finding a needle in a haystack, more like looking for a grain of sand in an ocean. Maybe a shark had swallowed it. Still, we clutch at straws.

'Where in the harbour?'

Maybe it was just off Balmain. Maybe on my morning walks to the park that jutted out into the water I would find one small key washed up among the garbage and the flowers of the ebbing tide.

'Off the back of a night ferry to Manly, a haversackful. Trinkets, one after the other, sparkling in the wake.'

'You didn't keep anything? As a memento of the occasion?'

'We kept the money.'

I supposed that was memento enough. With that money you could buy as many gold keys as you wanted. But not the key the Chens wanted. Not the key that might save Alice. It was beyond my means to dredge the harbour, beyond anyone's means, even the Chens. They were on their own now, no gold key, no symbols of power. Merlin had left them.

'Are you still there?'

Yes, I was still here.

'I think it's time to go. There may be other sinners waiting.'

I smiled to myself. 'Aren't you going to give me absolution, Father?'

'Of course my child. I absolve thee in the name of the Father, Son and the Holy Ghost. For your penance say three Hail Marys and help an old lady across the street. Leave the church by the front entrance and don't look back. If you do you will be turned into a pillar of salt.'

I didn't look back. Not till I'd got out of the church. The light was off now; there were the odd individuals at prayer, the tourists. My confessor could have been any one of them. Slipped off his robes and resumed his normal life.

Carol would not be pleased. She would say I should have informed the police. They would have had a stake-out. He wouldn't have come. But I wouldn't be telling Carol.

I wondered how many other lives had been disrupted by that bank job. The simple twists of fate. They could at least have dumped what they didn't want somewhere accessible—in the middle of Martin Place for example.

I crossed the road and walked down to where my car was parked.

I opened the car door. A hand came towards my face with a white pad held in it. I felt my head being whacked back. I struggled, but there wasn't any point. I was going down fast. In those few seconds of struggle I remembered thinking—the last thing I remembered—where does someone get chloroform in this modern day and age?

I **had been** kidnapped and taken to Asia. There were voices around me speaking in a language I didn't understand, men's voices. How long had the trip taken? How many hours, days? Wherever we had landed it was dark, very dark. And soft.

Slowly my brain started to come on duty again. It was soft because I was lying on a mattress, feeling rather cramped. It was dark because it was night. No. My brain tried again. It was dark because there was something covering my eyes. I raised my hand to remove the encumbrance and though I hadn't intended it, the other hand came up too. This one didn't take so long to figure out—my hands were tied together. I also discovered now why I felt so stiff and cramped. My legs were bent and tied together as well. Trussed up like a chicken. I imagined I heard one clucking. My green hat was missing.

The blindfold was wrenched off. I blinked in the light which wasn't all that bright. The place looked familiar. I'd been here before. It was the snooker room in Cabramatta.

But nothing was the same. There were still lots of men about but now they were wearing white robes with red headbands. They didn't look like they were about to play snooker. They were lined up in various parts of the room. The tables were missing. No, not all of them. There was one at the end of the room. It was made up to look like an altar. A square-looking object had been placed on it and was covered by a red cloth with some sort of insignia.

There was something familiar about all this too. As if I'd seen a picture of it in a book. *Multitudes of virtuous men assemble* . . . None of these men looked particularly virtuous. Something to do with willows. Willow pattern plate? No. Cities. City of Willows. The Triad initiation ceremony.

And what was my place in all of this? *Registration of recruits . . . execution of traitors.* I had the feeling it was not registration of recruits.

In front of the altar sat the man in the black hat, the man I'd seen here at the snooker room and again at the Queen Street gallery. His walking-stick hung on the back of his chair. A look of extreme satisfaction spread over his face, including the skin graft.

He snapped his fingers. Two of the white robes came towards me. One of them was the man with no tie.

He and the other guy grabbed me under the arms and dragged me up to the man in the black hat.

He snapped his fingers again and the man with no tie handed him the walking-stick.

He extended the hooked end towards me and stuck it under my chin.

He chuckled. I was glad he was enjoying it because I certainly wasn't. 'We will not waste each other's time. Just a few simple questions then you will be free to leave.'

Sure, I thought.

His expression changed completely. 'Where is the key?' he hissed through his gold teeth.

'Search me.'

If he had been one of the white boys around town I would have had a backhander across the face, but the double meaning was lost on him.

'We have, and you do not appear to have it,' he said, sneering into my face, 'but you do know where it is, don't you!' Now the backhander came. This brought me out of my chloroform daze completely.

I burned with frustration, the frustration of having been hit and not being able to hit back. Not even being able to turn my head away because the walking-stick was rammed hard against my throat. Lurking somewhere beneath the frustration was fear.

An undercurrent that might take me out to sea altogether. I was alone here in the presence of my enemies. I could not afford to have fear working against me as well.

'It's not anywhere you can lay your hands on in a hurry.'

'Where is it?' Another slap across the face.

'It's irretrievable.'

'It's what?'

'No-one can get it, not me, not you, not the Chens.'

'But you know where it is, don't you?'

I tried to turn my face but caught the slap anyway. I wished he'd stop doing that. From my point of view it was unnecessary and not very manly. And it was beginning to smart.

Now he bent down close to me, so close I could see the tiny black points of his close shave. He spoke carefully and slowly, weighing each of the words: 'If you want the child to live, you will tell us where the key is.'

My hands formed fists and came abruptly up under his chin, making him bite down on his tongue. He cursed and spat in my face. I smelled blood in the spit.

He removed the walking-stick from my chin and waved it towards the door. Two lackeys left the room. I hoped that meant he was going to stop slapping me around. It didn't. He asked the same question, I gave the same answer and received the slap.

The lackeys came back. With Alice. She was neatly dressed and clean, and her hair was tied up in a bow. She was carrying her doll. A big doll, almost as tall as she was. It had only one arm.

'Hello, Alice.' I hoped I spoke gently.

Another slap. 'You don't speak unless it is to tell us where the key is!'

Alice blinked but her face was stalwart.

'The key in exchange for the child. No key, no child.'

The lackeys placed heavy restraining hands on the child's shoulders.

'You understand?' he said with a victorious grin. 'Now, I will ask you again. Each time you give a wrong answer one of Alice's fingers will disappear; click!'

It was not necessary for him to click his fingers for me to understand his meaning.

'Let Alice go first.'

The slapper chuckled. 'Not so easy. A child might come to harm wandering the streets alone. The city is not a safe place.'

'Take her back to her grandmother. You've got cars, haven't you?'

The slapper gave a slight nod of his head. The lackey on Alice's left held her hand; a comforting gesture. He bounced it up and down a little then with one swift movement cracked her little finger out of joint.

Alice's face screwed up and she let out a wail that would have broken the heart of anyone in the room—if they had one. No-one budged or flinched. It looked like I was the only contender.

A woman entered the room. Two more of the white robes moved quickly to stand either side of her. I looked at her in surprise. It was the woman I'd seen leaving James Ho's room. Who had also been at the gallery with my interrogator.

The man with no tie, the man in the black hat and now the woman. All present and assembled. I scanned the faces of the men in white robes. The only person missing from the scene was James Ho.

James Ho. Willing to exchange six thousand years of civilisation for a description of the key. Who meant me no harm, who'd given me the false key to 'move things along'. Who'd staged the fight at the Red Dragon to show me whose side he was on. Well, I knew now, and it wasn't mine.

The man in the black hat was leering at me again.

'You seem to have some difficulty telling me the whereabouts of the key. I will try something simpler.' He applied further pressure to the walking-stick. I tried to swallow but couldn't. He bent down very close to me, so close that I could feel his clammy breath on my cheek. 'What does the key look like?'

'It's got a dragon on it.'

I wasn't giving anything away. Ho already knew about the dragon.

'And what else?' His voice dropped now to a malicious whisper. 'How does it open the boxes?'

I saw very clearly the photo of the key—the tubular shaft, the dragon and the six strangely shaped teeth. The clue to unlocking the boxes was the key. But which part of it?

'I don't know.'

He chuckled again. 'A great pity. Because you are going to open the boxes without the key.'

He removed the walking-stick from my throat and leant on it. I took a few deep breaths. He walked the few steps to the table and with a flourish removed the red cloth from the square-shaped object.

All eyes turned towards it, including mine. I almost gasped.

Beneath the cloth was a box, not unlike the cabinets at the gallery but infinitely more dazzling. Inlaid into silver were dragons. Their eyes were pearls, and each individual scale of their bodies was a flake of pure gold, thousands of them. It must have been worth an emperor's ransom.

'I see you like my treasure,' said the man in the black hat. 'Now you are going to reveal to me the treasure inside.' His smooth tones turned back to menace. 'Tell me how the key opens the box!'

Another slap across the face.

'I don't know!' I shouted, 'I don't know!'

He snapped his fingers again and once more the lackey started jiggling Alice's hand.

'If you know where the key is,' said the woman, 'please tell them.'

I looked at her and I looked at Alice. At Alice's eyes begging, pleading, please tell them. The lackey was watching me, still jiggling Alice's hand. I looked around the room, at the man in the black hat, at the others. They were all watching me. Waiting, waiting.

I had one chance and I had to make that chance work.

'St Marys Cathedral. The confessional on the eastern side, in the Bible, Exodus,' I whispered.

It wasn't hard to fake my sense of defeat.

The man in the black hat raised the walking-stick and brought it down across my temple. That did it. I passed out again.

When I came to this time my head felt like it was in a vice and I could smell haystacks. I opened my eyes. I was lying on seagrass matting, in a room the size of a cupboard. A knifeblade of light came from under the door. I edged my way over to it, raised my arms as best I could and very slowly tried the door handle. The door was locked. This came as no great surprise.

I heard voices outside and quickly resumed my unconscious position. The voices faded away.

I became aware of other voices. From below. I lifted the edge of the seagrass matting. There were floorboards underneath, some of which had cracks between them. I put my eye to a crack and looked down. Immediately below was the box with the gold dragons, covered again with the red cloth. But things had changed.

In front of the altar was my interrogator, dressed in a red robe. As well as the cloth-covered box, there was a red tub full of rice on the altar, a red club, a sword, a bloodstained robe, and what looked like a rosary.

Everyone looked to a part of the room I couldn't see, then an official-looking gentleman on the left of the altar started speaking, an intonation. The Incense Master. Something else happened out of range then the Incense Master went to the altar and lit five incense sticks. He started intoning again.

Fascinating as all this was I had a more pressing need—to get the hell out of here. My hands and feet were bound with plastic strips in a variety of knots a sailor would be proud of. They were the sort of plastic strips that make up banana chairs. I wondered whether the guard was still on the other side of the door and how often he looked in. Using the zipper of my jacket I tried to saw through the bindings. This was not easy. I couldn't hold the zipper out rigid and saw at the same time. I moved my hands up to my mouth and started to gnaw at the plastic like a mouse. It was wound round my hands six or seven times.

Five minutes had passed and I'd scarcely made a dent in it. It was going to be a long process. I hoped the initiation ceremony was also.

I looked below again. Now two men were kneeling before the altar holding incense sticks. My interrogator touched their backs with the sword and asked them a question. They gave a reply. I went back to gnawing at the plastic. I heard a chicken clucking and a final squawk. I looked down again to see the chicken lying on the altar. Its head was on the floor. They dripped its blood into a bowl then pricked the middle fingers of the two candidates and added human blood to the bowl. They took this communion offering and drank.

I chewed and gnawed and bit and nibbled. Eventually I got through the first loop. I had some mad hope that the whole thing might unravel but it didn't.

There was a soft exchange of voices outside then I heard a thud against the door. I heard someone fiddling with the lock. I moved over to the door ready to butt it back into the face of the first person who tried to walk in. The door opened a fraction, nowhere near enough to have any impact if I butted it.

Then I saw the shoes. The door opened wide and in stepped James Ho.

'Bastard!' I hissed at him.

He clapped his hand over my mouth and took out a knife.

A Swiss Army penknife.

And started cutting through the binding.

'Shame to do it really,' he whispered, 'you look so attractive tied up.'

He put the forefinger of one hand to his lips and with the other pointed to the room below.

'They are going to kill you,' he whispered, 'key or no key.'

Surprise, surprise, I thought, rubbing my wrists.

He dragged the guard in, a dead weight who offered no resistance. 'Put his clothes on then we'll tie him up.'

'Why?'

'You're less likely to be conspicuous.'

'You don't think a tall redheaded woman walking round in clothes that are too small for her is going to be conspicuous?' I whispered. 'Besides, I don't aim for them to see me. I'm going to find Alice then I'm out of here.'

'Maybe Alice doesn't want to go.'

'What?'

'Back to Mrs Chen.'

'Well she certainly won't be wanting to stay here. Do you know where Alice is?'

'Yes, in a room downstairs. After the ceremony the custom is to have a meal, a big dinner party. Considering the present circumstances I don't think they'll be doing that. Probably just have a cup of tea to while away the minutes till their men get back and tell the boss that the key wasn't where you said it was.'

'How did you know that?'

'I look, I listen.'

'Pity you didn't perform some actions as well. Might have saved the present state of my head.'

'I thought you didn't like me interfering in your business.'

'Hasn't stopped you before,' I muttered.

'During the ceremony the place is bristling with guards. But afterwards,' he said, gesturing elegantly, 'there's nothing for uninitiated eyes to see. You can't see anything; you're unconscious and tied up in a room. What fear do these men have of a mere woman?'

'I'm not mere.'

He was right about nearly everything. The place no longer bristled with guards, in fact the whole floor was now deserted. As we got to the window at the end of the hall I heard my interrogator make a short speech, followed by the clink of teacups. Toasting the new Triad members. There were stairs this end of the hall. Ho moved his head in the direction of the stairs. The room where Alice was being held was down there.

We dallied at the top of the staircase, trying to ascertain what might be happening down below. It was just as well, because in those few moments we heard voices. Ho pointed two fingers down the stairs then made tea-drinking movements with his hand. Very nice. Two guards downstairs were drinking tea.

But it told me more than that.

If we were going to make a move now was as good a time as any. We might get tea thrown in our faces but if it was cool enough to drink, it wasn't going to do much more damage to my already aching face.

I lay down on the floor and inched my way into a viewing position. One of the guards looked like he ate gorilla steaks for breakfast. The other one looked more manageable. They were bearing no visible weapons.

'Don't like yours much,' I said to James out of the side of my mouth.

'Piece of piss,' he said without even looking. It didn't suit him—'piece of piss'—but something rubs off if you stay in a country long enough.

I made a slight head movement indicating 'ready'.

Now!

Ho took three steps. One to spring up on the banister, one down it, and the third step was on the gorilla-eater's face. I was about two seconds behind on the other banister, similarly landing a boot in my opponent's face. One teacup, then the other, barely made a sound as they hit the carpet.

I clamped the guard's jaw shut so he couldn't call out. I slammed my knee up into his groin. Then I saw Ho's hands come round the guard's neck. He pressed with his thumbs on points either side of the neck near the jugular. In less than five seconds my guard had joined his mate on the floor.

I swallowed hard and involuntarily put my hand up to my own neck. It was feeling very tender. Meanwhile Ho was busy at work with a piece of wire in the keyhole of the door. He straightened up. We looked at each other and the corners of his mouth slid into the faintest of smiles. He opened the door and we went in.

I'd expected to find Alice in there, but not the woman. She was holding Alice and crying silently. Somehow she too had become a prisoner. She seemed to recognise Ho but she didn't speak. We could hear the men outside. There wasn't much time before the others would be back from St Marys bearing bad tidings.

We ushered the woman and child out and silently closed the

door behind us. The guards looked quite peaceful lying on the carpet but it wouldn't be long before they were up on their feet and roaring like bulls. We crept along the corridor and out the back door.

We came out into a yard surrounded by a brick wall with a tiled trim. The lawn was threadbare. If they were trying to make this look like the Sze Yap temple in Glebe they'd have to do much better.

I went over the wall first. Next Alice was hoisted over and then the woman. She wasn't really dressed for it but she did it elegantly.

We were barely over the wall when a car came spurting into the otherwise quiet Cabramatta back street. Suddenly the area was filled with noise.

The car screeched to a halt almost on top of us and two men leapt out, screaming like demons. They tried to grab Alice but before a hand was laid on her I kicked it away. I stuck my elbow into the face of one guy and swung around to deal with the other. But Ho was already dealing with him. The street bristled with activity as the men from the tea party came running towards us. My interrogator with his walking-stick was not one of them.

'Into the car,' I said to Alice and the woman. 'And lock the doors!' I yelled, as one of the guys dived for the car. I pushed him aside and leapt into the driver's seat and started the engine. 'Get in!' I yelled to Ho. 'You're not going to be able to deal with them all single-handedly.' Though I thought he probably could. 'Watch out!' I yelled as the guy on the ground made a grab for Ho's feet.

Ho slid into the car and slammed the door. On the guy's hand. I felt the bumps as the car went over something lumpy. I had a pretty good idea of what it was and I didn't want to look back. I took the corner on two wheels. We were four blocks away before the smell of burning rubber and flesh subsided.

But, as Collier would say, we were in no way home and hosed. Ho wanted to go back to the snooker room—'to pick up the boxes,' he said, as if it would be as easy as picking up laundry. Now was as good a time as ever. They would be out searching the streets for us. The last place they'd expect us to go was back to the snooker room. But my instincts were to get as far away from Cabramatta as possible. I didn't even have time to slow down to let Ho out. By the time we drove across the railway we were being tailed.

A red Torana and none too subtle about it either. He was belting through the traffic like his bum was on fire. And very soon, if he caught up, mine would be too. I turned off the Hume Highway and headed into Bankstown where there were lots more streets to hide in.

When we got into the main drag of Bankstown I saw a familiar sign.

'OK,' I said to Ho, 'this is where you get to play the Karate Kid.
The rest of us are getting out and slipping into something a little less conspicuous.'

The woman's body tightened. She looked at Ho. He said something that seemed to satisfy her. She got out of the car holding Alice's undamaged hand.

'In here,' I said, indicating the door of the rent-a-car office. 'Quickly.'

Ho drove off down the street. I ushered Alice and the woman to the back of the office, where they couldn't be seen from outside. I watched the window. The red Torana flashed by. It didn't double back.

'We'd like to hire a car for twenty-four hours,' I said, as calmly as I could to the perfectly groomed girl in the red and white-uniform.

She looked at me quizzically, then at Alice and the woman, trying to sum up the situation.

'A fast one,' I said, nudging things along.

She got out the forms. The preliminaries went smoothly till we got to the bit about the driver's licence. I felt in my pockets. There was nothing. Not even one of my calling cards. The Triad guys had cleaned me out.

'Got a driver's licence?' I asked the woman.

She shook her head.

'Look,' I said to the red and white girl, 'I know this is somewhat irregular but it is something of an emergency. Will you call your Kings Cross branch and speak to Sharon?'

'It's nearly closing time, madam.'

'I know, but I think Sharon will still be there.'

She smiled politely. After all, I was a customer.

She pursed her lips and dialled the number. 'Sharon please.'

It must have been Sharon who answered the phone because the girl started speaking right away. 'This is Monica from the Bankstown branch. We have a customer here,' she consulted the form I'd filled in, 'Claudia Valentine. Says she has some sort of regular arrangement with you.'

I smiled to myself. I used Sharon's cars a lot. My Daimler was often too easily identifiable. All but one car had been returned in the same condition I'd rented it. I was a good customer and Sharon knew that.

The girl's expression changed slightly. I don't know what Sharon was telling her but it was enough to get me a car.

It was a dark green Rover Vitesse, built for speed. The woman got into the back seat with Alice. I supposed she was used to being chauffeur-driven.

'You will drive us to the Airport Hilton hotel,' she said. She was used to giving orders to chauffeurs as well. 'You will arrange for Charles to come there. Alone, without his mother.'

Now I knew who she was. I turned around and looked at her steadily. There was a slight movement of the eyelids and she said, 'James will explain everything.'

'And if he doesn't make it back?'

'He will.'

As we headed back towards the highway I saw a police car pulled up at the side of the road. They were booking the driver of the red Torana. He looked extremely irate. I couldn't help smiling.

We drove to the airport in silence. Night surrounded us now, punctuated by the glow of streetlights. There were few cars about and none of them were following us.

You couldn't miss the Airport Hilton even if you tried. It stuck out like a boulder in the desert, out of place here, as if it should have been in the city with its tall brothers and sisters, not in the flat land that surrounded the airport.

The foyer was like any hotel foyer in the city: mirrors, lavishness and employees who looked like this was only a fill-in job till they made it big in the movies. There were more of them about now than there had been during my previous visit in the middle of the night.

Once inside the hotel the woman took the lead and she knew exactly what she was doing. There was something about her that reminded me of Mrs Chen, the same detachment, the same air of self-assurance. I wondered where you bought it.

The guy at reception handed her a square of plastic with 707 on it and a key dangling down.

'Thank you,' she said.

I'd waited outside room 707 what now seemed like an eternity ago. It was a suite in apricot colours, wardrobe doors with mirrors on the outside, a fake marble-top table with bandy gilt legs.

Alice looked around at everything, her eyes opening wide but her mouth remaining shut. I didn't know if she was a naturally quiet child or whether she was in shock. I smiled at her. I'm sorry, Alice, sorry for all of this. She looked at me but her expression didn't change.

'Please ring Charles,' the woman said simply.

I went to the phone and the woman went to the fridge. I hoped she was going to make us a couple of stiff Scotches.

I rang the Chen residence and spoke to Charles. I was brief and to the point. 'Airport Hilton, room 707. Come alone and make sure you're not followed. And Charles, there's no need to concern your mother in this matter.' I hung up. There was nothing to do but wait.

The woman wasn't making Scotches, she was making an ice pack for Alice's hand. She took Alice into the bedroom and talked softly to her. Still Alice's expression didn't change.

I felt suddenly very tired. But if I lay down now I might never get up again.

I went into the bathroom, grey-blue tiles with gold taps. There was only one toothbrush, and an electric shaver. I didn't think it belonged to the woman. I wondered how many other rooms around the town James Ho had shavers in.

There were lots of mirrors in the bathroom. The one above the handbasin had gilt round its edges. The face staring back at me from that mirror wasn't looking good. It was starting to show some maroon-coloured patches. I could vaguely discern in those patches the shape of my interrogator's hand.

I ran the cold tap and sluiced water on my face, patting it gingerly with the apricot-coloured towel.

I came back out again. 'Would you like a drink?' I called.

The woman said no, but asked if I could get an orange juice for Alice.

I'd just finished pouring the juice when there was a soft knock on the door. I went and opened it a fraction. Satisfied, I opened the door fully and in walked Charles Chen.

The woman appeared from the bedroom, standing demurely with her hands behind her back. He looked at her as if she was a vision from another world. I don't think it was simply the halo effect the lamp was creating around her.

'Tai May!'

'Good evening, Charles.'

He started to advance towards her. She held her ground.

'Where's Alice? What have you done with her?'

'Alice is here, she's safe. I'm pleased to see you are showing some concern. More concern than you showed seven years ago. For me or Alice.'

'I'm taking her home.' Charles stepped towards the bedroom. Only one step then he halted abruptly.

'No, Charles,' said the woman, 'I am taking her home.' Both her hands were now visible. In one of them was a gun.

The moment froze. Charles stood there gaping, his mouth open.

Finally he spoke.

'You're not taking Alice out of the country. What sort of life can you offer her?'

'A better one than she has with your mother.' Each word leaden and as penetrating as a bullet.

'Why didn't you contact me?' asked Charles, with a weakness born of despair.

'Your mother would never have let me near Alice. You know that.'

'Perhaps I could have intervened.'

He didn't convince me.

'Sure, Charlie,' she said softly.

He hadn't convinced her either.

She faltered a little, looking at the boy whose first love she had been, some love in her business of sex.

'I need time with her,' she said, imploring. 'I've waited seven years for my child. I am her mother. She will love me. Give me this time, Charles.'

'Kidnapping is no way to win her.'

'She was well looked after.'

I thought of the broken finger. Sure. You play with crims, you get caught in the crossfire.

'Your mother took her from me. She had no right to Alice, no right to my child.'

'Alice is loved,' said Charles.

'Yes, and locked up in a temple.'

'So you had her kidnapped.'

'Do you think I could simply go to your house and ask for my child? I have worked for this. Every minute of the last seven years has been devoted to getting Alice back. I have used your mother's money wisely. I have remade myself. I have made many important contacts. You remember the nights in my room in Kings Cross? You told me about the key; you thought it was stupid Chinese superstition. I made investigations; I found the men who wanted the power of the key. I told them I knew a way to get it.'

'You put your own child up for ransom.'

'No, Charles, I bought her back.'

She carefully backed into the bedroom and picked up the child, speaking to her in soothing tones. Then she picked up a large handbag. Charles made another move towards the bedroom. 'I am taking my daughter home,' said Tai May. 'I do not think you will stop me.'

I didn't think he'd stop her. Not with a gun pointed at him.

'The keys to the car,' she said to me. 'Please put them carefully on the table.'

I did what I'd been told.

Tai May picked up the keys.

'Leaving without James?' I asked with as much sarcasm as I dared.

'I have Alice back, I no longer require his services. Open the door, Charles.'

He opened it.

'Stand away from it.'

He moved away.

'Do not try to follow.'

She went out the door and locked it behind her.

'Why didn't you try and stop her?' begged Charles.

He started ranging around the room. I wondered if he was going to tear his hair out.

'I don't like the nasty little imprint bullets leave. Besides, Alice probably has as much of a chance with Tai May as she has with your mother.'

He came back to the door, started banging on it, and shouting for help.

'Calm down, Charles,' I said. 'Why don't we just wait here quietly till the plane takes off? James Ho will be here in a minute. With the boxes your key opens. You should find him interesting. He knows all about silly old Chinese superstitions.'

'My mother will be here in a minute as well,' beamed Charles, triumphant.

I should have guessed. Those apron strings were too tightly bound for someone like Charles to break free of them. His one big chance and he blew it.

'Well, we'll want to be able to let her in, won't we?'

I phoned the desk and asked them to come up to room 707. We'd been inadvertently locked in, I explained.

'Now let's sit down and have a drink. Orange juice or Scotch?' I asked, getting the drinks that were still on top of the fridge.

'Scotch,' murmured Charles, slumping into the apricot-coloured lounge chair.

It wasn't long before the hotel people were at the door unlocking it.

'Thank you,' I said.

The guy walked away.

'Sorry about this, Charles, but I have to go. Enjoy your drink.'

I quickly moved out into the corridor and locked the door behind me. I had to get to the airport, and in a hurry. I had a feeling Mrs Chen might bypass Charles and go straight for Alice.

I took the lift down to the foyer and got in a waiting cab.

'Airport.'

The driver nodded and slowly started to pull out of the driveway.

'Can you speed it up a little?' I said. 'I've got a plane to catch.'

'With no luggage?'
'That's right. No luggage.'

The departure lounge was full of the usual mixed feelings, those who wanted to go and those who didn't want them to go. Young backpackers out to conquer the world, full of high hopes and expectation, businessmen and women with bland expressions.

I looked at the board indicating departures. There was a flight for Singapore now boarding.

Gate number six.

I bounded up the escalator.

Towards the end of the hall I could see the queue at passport control. Tai May was there with Alice.

But I was too late. Ahead of me, running towards the queue as fast as her high heels would allow, was Mrs Chen. And the chauffeur of the white Mercedes.

I ran, and watched Mrs Chen draw level with the queue. I started to call out. Then I stopped.

Everything stopped.

Mrs Chen reached her hand out to Alice. I heard the shot then saw Mrs Chen stagger back. There was a small round hole in the front of her blue dress just starting to show a trickle of blood.

Maybe I had expected her to go down in swirls of smoke and flame, the earth to cave in and buildings come tumbling down, but Mrs Chen just teetered backwards and slumped inelegantly to the ground, her foot twisted at an odd angle.

Tai May looked at the gun in her hand as if wondering how it had got there.

Then the security guards moved in, obscuring my view.

Carol wanted to know what all this had to do with the Chinatown bank robbery. I told her it had nothing to do with it. She wanted to know how my investigations were going in that department. I told her the trail was dead. She said she believed I was holding out on her. I said she could believe what she liked. She asked me about the child. I said she was now with her father. She asked me what had happened to my Chinese friend. I said I'd lost track of him. She asked me what I was doing at the airport in the first place. I told her I like to get lost in the crowd. She told me to keep myself available for further questioning. I said yes, I would do that.

POSTSCRIPT

Hong Kong
24 April 1988

Dearest Claudia,

My humble apologies for not having said goodbye to you before I left your country but, let's say, my visa expired rather suddenly and I did not want to over-stay.

I had a very interesting talk with Charles Chen, whom I found in my hotel room when I returned from Cabramatta with the boxes. I had been hoping to find you. It could have been the continuation of a beautiful friendship. The boxes were a great help in convincing him that the story of the key was not simply superstition, and he kindly promised to send me its photograph. He was surprised that you hadn't mentioned its existence to me. Knowing you as I do from our brief but exciting encounters, I was not surprised.

So, you see, I managed to get not only a detailed description of the key but photographic evidence, in spite of your obstinacy about this matter. My father has examined the evidence closely and has had some success.

He has opened the first box.

Am I arousing your curiosity? I had hoped to arouse you in other ways, at your leisure. But I digress.

The clue to opening the boxes is in the six protrusions. Minutely inscribed on them are ancient Chinese symbols, similar to those found on oracle bones. My father finally deciphered them.

Pressing simultaneously on the pearl eyes of one of the dragons unlatches the first box.

But unfortunately, it seems that each box opens in a different way. My father has pressed and prodded but to no avail. And of course the photo is two-dimensional. We need to see the symbols on the other side of the protrusions to unlock the rest of the boxes.

For that we need the key itself.

We would like you to continue your search for it. I'm sure we could come to a happy arrangement, financial or otherwise. If fortune doesn't appeal to you, perhaps fame does. You could go down in history as the woman who solved the case of the Chinese boxes.

Your partner in puzzle solving,

James Ho

Sydney,
15 May 1988

Dear James,

I'm glad your stay here was so fruitful, and I don't just mean the figs. If you're ever over this way again give me a call. And I do mean call rather than just popping in.

If you've been in contact with Charles you probably already know that Tai May is standing trial for the murder of Victoria Chen. She is pleading extenuating circumstances and has named our Cabramatta friends, but they seem to have left the country. Keep an eye out, James Ho, they may turn up on your turf.

Nearly six months further down the track and still none of the bank robbery items have turned up. This includes the key. A reliable informant tells me the key is irretrievable, out of reach of anyone, of you or me.

And I'm not interested any more, nothing is worth that kind of trouble.

So you see, James, your offer of fame or fortune is an offer that I'll have to refuse.

As far as I'm concerned the case is now closed.

Your partner in puzzle solving,

Claudia Valentine

PS: If you do come to Sydney again could you bring me a pair of those Italian leather shoes? I take size 7 and I like red.

THE LIFE AND CRIMES OF HARRY LAVENDER

MARELE DAY

Mark Bannister is writing 'the bestseller of the century'. But when he's found dead at his computer he seems to be the victim of a murder so perfect that Claudia Valentine smells a rat – and wants it caught.

The chase leads deep into Sydney's murky underworld – a world where bright, tough Claudia must play a deadly high-tech game of cat and rat with the menacing overlord of the city's cancerous network of crime and corruption.

Witty, wry and fast-paced, THE LIFE AND CRIMES OF HARRY LAVENDER is a thriller with a twist and a crime novel which brilliantly evokes the sleaze beneath the surface of a city's glittering facade.

'Exciting, fast-paced and plenty of just slightly shabby style – in fact everything a good detective yarn should be'

The Daily Telegraph

HODDER AND STOUGHTON PAPERBACKS